Mystery Stories for Boys

Triple Spies

Mystery Stories for Boys

Triple Spies

Roy J. Snell

1920

TRIPLE SPIES

Published in the United States by IndyPublish.com
Boston, Massachusetts

ISBN 1-4142-5599-3 (hardcover)
ISBN 1-4142-5600-0 (paperback)

CONTENTS

CHAPTER I

THE DEN OF DISGUISES

As Johnny Thompson stood in the dark doorway of the gray stone court-yard he shivered. He was not cold, though this was Siberia—Vladivostok—and a late winter night. But he was excited.

Before him, slipping, sliding, rolling over and over on the hard packed snow of the narrow street, two men were gripped in a life and death struggle. They had been struggling thus for five minutes, each striving for the upper hand. The clock in the Greek Catholic church across the way told Johnny how long they had fought.

He had been an accidental and entirely disinterested witness. He knew neither of the men; he had merely happened along just when the row began, and had lingered in the shadows to see it through. Twelve, yes, even six months before, he would have mixed in at once; that had always been his way in the States. Not that he was a quarrelsome fellow; on the contrary he was fond of peace, was Johnny, in spite of the fact that he carried on his person various medals for rather more-than-good feather-weight fighting. He loved peace so much that he was willing to lick almost anyone in order to make them stop fighting. That was why he had joined the American army, and allowed himself to be made part of the Expeditionary force that went to the Pacific coast side of Siberia.

But twelve months in Siberia had taught him many things. He had learned that he could not get these Russians to stop quarreling by merely whipping them. Therefore, since these men were both Russians, he had let them fight.

The tall, slender man had started it. He had rushed at the short, square shouldered one from the dark. The square shouldered one had flashed a knife. This had
been instantly knocked from his grasp. By some chance, the knife had dropped
only an arm's length from the doorway into which Johnny had dodged. Johnny
now held the knife discreetly behind his back.

Yes, Johnny trembled. There was a reason for that. The tall, slender man had
gained the upper hand. He was stretched across the prone form of his antagonist,
his slim, horny hands even now gliding toward the other's throat. And, right
there, Johnny had decided to draw the line. He was not going to allow himself to
witness the strangling of a man. That wasn't his idea of fighting. He would end
the fight, even at the expense of being mussed up a bit himself, or having certain
of his cherished plans interfered with by being dragged before a "Provo" as witness or participant.

He was counting in a half-audible whisper, "Forty-one, forty-two, forty-three." It
was a way he had when something big was about to happen. The hand of the slender man was at the second button on the other's rough coat when Johnny reached
fifty. At sixty it had come to the top button. At sixty-five his long finger-tips were
doubling in for the fatal, vice-like grip. Noiselessly, Johnny laid the knife on a
cross bar of the door. Knives were too deadly. Johnny's "wallop" was quite enough;
more than enough, as the slender one might learn to his sorrow.

But before Johnny could move a convulsion shot through the prostrate fighter.
He was again struggling wildly. At the same instant, Johnny heard shuffling footsteps approaching around the corner. He was sure he did not mistake the tread of
Japanese military police who were guarding that section of the city. For a moment
he studied the probabilities of the short one's power of endurance, then, deciding
it sufficient to last until the police arrived, he gripped the knife behind his back
and darted toward an opposite corner where was an alley offering safety. There
were very definite reasons why Johnny did not wish to figure even as a witness in
any case in Vladivostok that night.

In a doorway off the alley, he paused, listening for sounds of increased tumult.
They came quickly enough. There was a renewed struggle, a grunt, a groan; then
the scuffling ceased.

Suddenly, a figure darted down the alley. Johnny caught a clear view of the man's
face. The fugitive was the shorter man with broad shoulders and sharp chin; the
man who the moment before had been the under dog. He was followed closely

by another runner, but not his antagonist in the street fight. This man was a Japanese; and Johnny saw to his surprise that the Jap did not wear the uniform of the military police; in fact, not any uniform at all.

"Evidently, that stubby Russian with the queer chin is wanted for something," Johnny muttered. "I wonder what. Anyway, I've got his knife."

At that he tucked the weapon beneath his squirrel-lined coat and, dropping out of his corner, went cautiously on his way.

So eager was he to attend to other matters that the episode of the street fight was soon forgotten. Dodging around this corner, then that, giving a wide berth to a group of American non-coms, dashing off a hasty salute to three Japanese officers, he at last turned up a narrow alley, and, with a sigh of relief, gave three sharp raps, then a muffled one, at a door half hidden in the gloom.

The door opened a crack, and a pair of squint eyes studied him cautiously.

"Ow!" said the yellow man, opening the door wider, and then closing it almost before Johnny could crowd himself inside.

To one coming from the outer air, the reeking atmosphere within this low ceilinged, narrow room was stifling. There was a blend of vile odors; opium smoke, not too ancient in origin, mixed with smells of cooking, while an ill-defined but all-pervading odor permeated the place; such an odor as one finds in a tailor's repair shop, or in the place of a dealer in second-hand clothing.

Second-hand clothing, that was Wo Cheng's line. But it was a rather unusual shop he kept. Being a Chinaman, he could adapt himself to circumstances, at least within his own realm, which was clothes. His establishment had grown up out of the grim necessity and dire pressure of war. Not that the pressure was on his own person; far from that. Somewhere back in China this crafty fellow was accumulating a fortune. He was making it in this dim, taper-lighted, secret shop, opening off an alley in Vladivostok.

In these times of shifting scenes, when the rich of to-day were the poor of to-morrow, or at least were under the necessity of feigning poverty, there were many people who wished to change their station in life, and that very quickly. It was Wo Cheng's business to help them make this change. Many a Russian noble had sought this noisome shop to exchange his "purple and fine linen" for very humble garb, and just what he took from the pockets of one and put in the pockets of the other suit, Wo Cheng had a way of guessing, though he appeared not to see at all.

Johnny had known Wo Cheng for some time. He had discovered his shop by accident when out scouting for billets for American soldiers. He had later assisted in protecting the place from a raid by Japanese military police.

"You wanchee somsling?" The Oriental grinned, as Johnny seated himself cross-legged on a grass mat.

"Yep," Johnny grinned in return, "wanchee change." He gripped the lapel of his blouse, as if he would remove it and exchange for another.

"You wanchee clange?" The Chinaman squinted at him with an air of incredulity.

Then a light of understanding seemed to over-spread his face. "Ow!" he exclaimed, "no can do, Mellican officer, not any. No can do."

"Wo Cheng, you no savvy," answered Johnny, glancing about at the tiers of costumes which hung on either side of the wall.

"Savvy! Savvy!" exclaimed Wo Cheng, bounding away to return with the uniform of an American private. "Officer, all same," he exclaimed. "No can do."

"No good," said Johnny, starting up. "You no savvy. Mebby you no wanchee savvy. No wanchee uniform. Wanchee clothes, fur, fur, plenty warm, you savvy? Go north, north, cold, savvy?"

"Ow!" exclaimed the Chinaman, scratching his head.

"Wo Cheng!" said Johnny solemnly, "long time my see you. Allatime, my see you. Not speak American Major; not speak Japanese police."

Wo Cheng shivered.

"Now," said Johnny, "my come buy."

"Ow!" grunted Wo Cheng, ducking from sight and reappearing quickly with a great coat of real seal, trimmed with sea otter, a trifle which had cost some noble of other days a king's ransom.

"No wanchee," Johnny shook his head.

"Ow!" Wo Cheng shook his head incredulously. This was his rarest offering. "You no got cumshaw, money?" he grinned. "All wite, my say."

"No wanchee my," Johnny repeated.

The Chinaman took the garment away, and returned with a similar one, less pretentious. This, too, was waved aside.

By this time Johnny had become impatient. Time was passing. A special train was to go north at four o'clock. It was going for reindeer meat, rations for the regiment that was Johnny's, or, at least, had been Johnny's. He could catch a ride on that train. A five hundred mile lift on a three thousand mile jaunt was not to be missed just because this Chink was something of a blockhead.

Pushing the proprietor gently to one side, Johnny made his way toward the back of the room. Scrutinizing the hangers as he went, and giving them an occasional fling here and there, as some garment caught his eye, he came presently upon a solid square yard of fur. With a grunt of satisfaction, he dragged one of the garments from its place and held it before the flickering yellow taper.

The thing was shaped like a middy-blouse, only a little longer and it had a hood attached. It was made of the gray squirrel skins of Siberia, and was trimmed with wolf's skin. As Johnny held it against his body, it reached to his knees. It was, in fact, a parka, such as is worn by the Eskimos of Alaska and the Chukches, aborigines of North Siberia.

One by one, Johnny dragged similar garments from their hangers. Coming at last upon one made of the brown summer skins of reindeer, and trimmed with wolverine, he seemed satisfied, for, tossing the others into a pile, he had drawn off his blouse and was about to throw the parka over his head, when something fell with a jangling rattle to the floor.

"O-o-ee!" grunted the Chinaman, as he stared at the thing. It was the knife which had belonged to the Russian of the broad shoulders and sharp chin. As Johnny's eyes fell upon it now, he realized that it was an altogether unusual weapon. The blade was of blue steel, and from its ring it appeared to be exceptionally well tempered. The handle was of strangely carved ivory.

Quickly thrusting the knife beneath his belt, Johnny again took up the parka. This time, as he drew the garment down over his head, he appeared to experience considerable difficulty in getting his left arm into the sleeve. This task accomplished, he stretched himself this way and that. He smoothed down the fur thoughtfully, pulled the hood about his ears, and back again, twisted himself about to test the fit, then, with a sigh of content, turned to examine a pile of fur trousers.

At that instant there came a low rap at the door—three raps, to be accurate—then a muffled thud.

Johnny started. Someone wanted to enter. He was not exactly in a condition to be seen, especially if the person should prove to be an American officer. His fur parka, topping those khaki trousers and puttees of his, would seem at least to tell a tale, and might complicate matters considerably. Quickly seizing his blouse, he crowded his way far back into the depths of a furry mass of long coats.

"Wo Cheng!" he whispered, "my wanchee you keep mouth shut. Allatime shut!"

"O-o-ee," grunted the Chinaman.

The next moment he had opened the door a crack.

The squint eyes of the Chinaman surveyed the person without for a long time, so long, in fact, that Johnny began to wonder what sort of person the newcomer could be. Wo Cheng was keen of wit. To many he refused entrance. But he was also a keen trader. All manner of men and women came to him; some for a permanent change of costume, some for a night's exchange only. Peasants, grown suddenly and strangely rich, bearing passports and tickets for other lands, came to buy the cast-off finery of the one time nobility. Russian, Japanese, American soldiers and officers came to Wo Cheng for a change, most of them for a single twelve hours, that they might revel in places forbidden to men in uniform. But some came for a permanent change. Wo Cheng never inquired why. He asked only "Cumshaw, money," and got it.

Was this newcomer Russian, Japanese, Chinaman or American?

The door at last opened half way, then closed quickly. The person who stood blinking in the light was not a man, but a woman, a short and slim young woman, with the dark round face of a Japanese.

"You come buy?" solicited Wo Cheng.

For answer, the woman drew off her outer garment of some strange wool texture and trimmed with ermine. Then, as if it were an everyday occurrence, she stepped out of her rich silk gown, and stood there in a suit of deep purple pajamas.

She then stared about the place until her eyes reached the fur garments which Johnny had recently examined. With a laugh and a spring, lithe as a panther, she seized upon one of these, then discarding it with a fling, delved deeper until she came upon some smaller garments, which might better fit her slight form. Comparing for a moment one of squirrel skin with one of fawn skin, she finally laid aside the latter. Then she attacked the pile of fur trousers. At the bottom she came upon some short bloomers, made also of fawn skin. With another little gurgle of laughter, she stepped into these. Next she drew the spotted fawn skin parka over her head, and stood there at last, the picture of a winsome Eskimo maid.

This done, woman-like, she plumed herself for a time before a murky mirror. Then, turning briskly, she slipped out of the garments and back into her own.

"You wanchee cumshaw?" she asked, handing the furs to the Chinaman to be wrapped.

The Chinaman grinned.

From somewhere on her person she extracted bills, American bills. Johnny was not surprised at that, for in these uncertain times, American money had come to be an undisputed medium of exchange. It was always worth as much to-day as yesterday—very often more. The thing that did surprise Johnny was the size of the bills she left with the dealer. She was buying those garments, there could be no question about that. But why? No one in this region would think of wearing them. They were seldom seen five hundred miles north. And this woman was a Japanese. There were no Japanese men at Khabarask, five hundred miles north, let alone Japanese women; Johnny knew that.

But the door had closed. The American looked at his watch. It was one o'clock. The train went at four. He must hurry.

He was about to move out from among the furs, when again there came a rap, this time loud and insistent, as if coming from one who was accustomed to be obeyed.

"American officer!" Johnny stifled a groan, as he slid back into hiding.

"Wo Cheng!" he cautioned again in a whisper, "my wanchee you keep mouth shut; you savvy?"

"O-o-ee," mumbled Wo Cheng, his hand on the latch.

CHAPTER II

THE MYSTERIOUS RUSSIAN

Johnny's jaw dropped, and he barely checked a gasp, as through his screen of furs he saw the man who now entered Wo Cheng's den of disguises. He was none other than the man of the street fight, the short one of the broad shoulders and sharp chin. Johnny was surprised in more ways than one; surprised that the man was here at all; that it could have been he who had given that authoritative signal at the door, and most of all, surprised that Wo Cheng should have admitted him so readily, and should be treating him with such deference.

"Evidently," Johnny thought to himself, "this fellow has been here before."

Although unquestionably a Russian, the newcomer appeared quite equal to the task of making his wants known in Chinese, for after a moment's conversation the two men made their way toward the back of the room.

Johnny had his second shock when he saw the garments the Russian began to examine. They were no other than those which had twice before in the last hour been examined by customers, the clothing for the Far North. This was too much. Again, he barely checked a gasp. Was the entire population of the city about to move to the polar regions? He would ask Wo Cheng. In the meantime, Johnny prayed that the Russian might make his choice speedily, since the time of departure of his train was approaching.

The Russian made his selections, apparently more from a sense of taste than with an eye to warmth and service. This final choice was a suit of squirrel skin and boots of deer skin.

"Cumshaw?"

Into Wo Cheng's beady, squinting eyes, as he addressed this word to the Russian, there came a look of malignant cunning which Johnny had not seen there before. It sent chills racing up and down his spine. It almost seemed to him that the Chinaman's hand was feeling for his belt, where his knife was hidden.

For a moment the Russian turned his back to Wo Cheng, and so faced Johnny. Behind his screen, the "Yank" could observe his actions without himself being seen.

From an inner pocket the Russian extracted a long, thick envelope. Unwrapping the cord at the top of this, he shook from it three shining particles.

"Diamonds!" Johnny's eyes were dazzled with the lustre of the jewels.

The Russian, selecting one, dropped the others back into the envelope.

"Bet he's got a hundred more," was Johnny's mental comment. Then he noticed a peculiarity of the envelope. There was a red circle in the lower, left hand corner, as if a seal had been stamped there. He would remember that envelope should he ever see it again.

But at this instant his attention was drawn to the men again. The Russian had turned and handed the gem to Wo Cheng. Wo Cheng stepped to the light and examined it.

"No need cumshaw my," he murmured.

The Russian bowed gravely, and turned toward the door.

It was then that the face of the Chinaman underwent a rapid change. The look of craftiness, treachery, and greed swept over it again. This time the yellow man's hand unmistakably reached for the knife.

Then he appeared to remember Johnny, for his hand dropped, and he half turned with an air of guilt.

The door closed with a little swish. The Russian was gone. With him went the stifling air of treachery, murder and intrigue, yet it left Johnny wondering. Why was every man's hand lifted against the sharp-chinned Russian? Had Wo Cheng been actuated by hate, or by greed? Johnny could not but wonder if some of Russia's former noblemen did not rest in shallow graves beneath Wo Cheng's cellar floor. But there was little time for speculation. In two hours the special train that Johnny wanted to take would be on its way north.

Springing nimbly from his place of hiding, Johnny recovered his blouse, and having secured from it certain papers, which were of the utmost importance to him, he pinned them in a pocket of his shirt. He next selected a pair of wolf skin trousers, a pair of corduroy trousers, one pair of deer skin boots and two of seal skin.

"Cumshaw?" he grinned, facing Wo Cheng, as he completed his selection.

The yellow man shrugged his shoulders, as if to say it made little difference to him in this case.

Johnny peeled a bill from his roll of United States currency and handed it to him.

"Wo Cheng," he said slowly, "go north, Jap woman? Go north, that Russian? Why?"

The Chinaman's face took on a mask-like appearance.

"No can do," he muttered. "Allatime keep mouth shut my."

"Tell me," commanded Johnny, advancing in a threatening manner, with his hand near the Russian's knife.

"No can do," protested the Chinaman cringing away. "Allatime keep mouth shut my. No ask my. No tell my. Allatime buy, sell my. No savvy my."

It was evident that nothing was to be learned here of the intentions of the two strangers; so, grasping his bundle, Johnny lifted the latch and found himself out in the silent, deserted alley.

The air was kind to his heated brow. As he took the first few steps his costume troubled him. He was wearing the parka and the corduroy trousers. He felt no longer the slight tug of puttees about his ankles. His trousers flapped against his legs at every step. The hood heated the back of his neck. The fur trousers and the skin boots were in the bundle under his arm. His soldier's uniform he had left with the keeper of the hidden clothes shop. He hardly thought that anyone, save a very personal acquaintance, would recognize him in his new garb, and there was little chance of such a meeting at this hour of the night. However, he gave three American officers, apparently returning from a late party of some sort, a wide berth, and dodging down a narrow street, made his way toward the railway yards where he would find the drowsy comforts of the caboose of the "Reindeer Special."

*   *   *   *   *

"American, ain't y'?" A sergeant of the United States army addressed this question to Johnny.

The latter was curled up half asleep in a corner of the caboose of the "Reindeer Special" which had been bumping over the rails for some time.

"Ya-a," he yawned.

"Going north to trade, I s'pose?"

Johnny was tempted not to answer. Still, he was not yet out of the woods.

"Yep," he replied cheerfully. "Red fox, white fox, mink, squirrel, ermine, muskrat. Mighty good price."

"Where's your pack?" The sergeant half grinned.

Johnny sat up and stared. No, it was not that he had had a pack and lost it. It was that he had never had a pack. And traders carried packs. Why to be sure; things to trade for furs.

"Pack?" he said confusedly. "Ah-er, yes. Why, yes, my pack, of course, why I left it; no—hang it! Come to think of it, I'm getting that at the end of this line, Khabarask, you know."

Johnny studied the old sergeant through narrowing eyelids. He had given him a ten spot before the train rattled from the yards. Was that enough? Would any sum be enough? Johnny shivered a little. The man was an old regular, a veteran of many battles not given in histories. Was he one of those who took this motto: "Anything's all right that you can get away with?" Johnny wondered. It might be, just might be, that Johnny would go back on this same train to Vladivostok; and that, Johnny had no desire to do.

The sergeant's eyes closed for a wink of sleep. Johnny looked furtively about the car. The three other occupants were asleep. He drew a fat roll of American bills from his pocket. From the very center he extracted a well worn one dollar bill. Having replaced the roll, he smoothed out the "one spot" and examined it closely. Across the face of it was a purple stamp. In the circle of this stamp were the words, "Wales, Alaska." A smile spread over Johnny's shrewd, young face.

"Yes sir, there you are, li'l ol' one-case note," he whispered. "You come all the way from God's country, from Alaska to Vladivostok, all by yourself. I don't know how many times you changed hands before you got here, but here you are, and it took you only four months to come. Stay with me, little old bit of Uncle Sam's treasure, and I'll take you home; straight back to God's country."

He folded the bill carefully and stowed it in an inner pocket, next to his heart.

If the missionary postmistress at Cape Prince of Wales, on Behring Strait, had realized what homesick feelings she was going to stir up in Johnny's heart by impressing her post office stamp on that bill before she paid it to some Eskimo, perhaps she would not have stamped it, and then again, perhaps she would.

A sudden jolt as they rumbled on to a sidetrack awoke the sergeant, who seemed disposed to resume the conversation where he had left off.

"S'pose it's mighty dangerous tradin' on this side?"

"Uh-huh," Johnny grunted.

"S'pose it's a long way back to God's country this way?"

"Uh-huh."

"Lot of the boys mighty sick of soldiering over here. Lot of 'em 'ud try it back to God's country 'f 'twasn't so far."

"Would, huh?" Johnny yawned.

"Ye-ah, and then the officers are mighty hard on the ones they ketch—ketch desertin', I mean—officers are; when they ketch 'em, an' they mostly do."

"Do what?" Johnny tried to yawn again.

"Ketch 'em! They're fierce at that."

There was a knowing grin on the sergeant's face, but no wink followed. Johnny waited anxiously for the wink.

"But it's tough, now ain't it?" observed the sergeant. "We can't go home and can't fight. What we here for, anyway?"

"Ye-ah," Johnny smiled hopefully.

"Expected to go home long ago, but no transportation, not before spring; not even for them that's got discharges and papers to go home. It's tough! You'd think a lot of 'em 'ud try goin' north to Alaska, wouldn't you? Three days in God's country's worth three years in Leavenworth; you'd think they'd try it. And they would, if 't wasn't so far. Gad! Three thousand miles! I'd admire the pluck of the fellow that dared."

This time the wink which Johnny had been so anxiously awaiting came; a full, free and frank wink it was. He winked back, then settled down in his corner to sleep.

A train rattled by. The "Reindeer Special" bumped back on the main track and went crashing on its way. It screeched through little villages, half buried in snow. It glided along between plains of whiteness. It rattled between narrow hills, but Johnny was unconscious of it all. He was fast asleep, storing up strength for the morrow, and the many wild to-morrows which were to follow.

CHAPTER III

TREACHERY OUT OF THE NIGHT

Johnny moved restlessly beneath his furs. He had been dreaming, and in his dream he had traveled far over scorching deserts, his steed a camel, his companions Arabs. In his dream he slept by night on the burning sand, with only a silken canopy above him. In his dream he had awakened with a sense of impending danger. A prowling tiger had wandered over the desert, an Arab had proved treacherous—who knows what? The feeling, after all, had been only of a vague dread.

The dream had wakened him, and now he lay staring into utter darkness and marveling that the dream was so much like the reality. He was traveling over barren wastes with a caravan; had been for three days. But the waste they crossed was a waste of snow. His companions were natives—who like the Arabs, lived a nomadic life. Their steeds the swift footed reindeer, their tents the igloos of walrus and reindeer skins, they roamed over a territory hundreds of miles in extent. To one of these "fleets of the frozen desert," Johnny had attached himself after leaving the train.

It had been a wonderful three days that he had spent in his journeying northward. These Chukches of Siberia, so like the Eskimos of Alaska that one could distinguish them only by the language they spoke, lived a romantic life. Johnny had entered into this life with all the zest of youth. True, he had found himself very awkward in many things and had been set aside with a growled, "Dezra" (that is enough), many times but he had persevered and had learned far more about the ways of these nomads of the great, white north than they themselves suspected.

During those three days Johnny's eyes had been always on the job. He had not traveled a dozen miles before he had made a thorough study of the reindeer equipment. This, indeed, was simple enough, but the simpler one's equipment, the more thorough must be one's knowledge of its handling. The harness of the deer was made of split walrus skin and wood. Simple wooden hames, cut to fit the shoulders of the deer and tied together with a leather thong, took the place of both collar and hames of other harnesses. From the bottom of these hames ran a broad strap of leather. This, passing between both the fore and hind legs of the deer, was fastened to the sled. A second broad strap was passed around the deer's body directly behind the fore legs. This held the pulling strap above the ground to prevent the reindeer from stepping over his trace. In travel, in spite of this precaution, the deer did often step over the trace. In such cases, the driver had but to seize the draw strap and give it a quick pull, sending the sled close to the deer's heels. This gave the draw straps slack and the deer stepped over the trace again to his proper place.

The sleds were made of a good quality of hard wood procured from the river forests or from the Russians, and fitted with shoes of steel or of walrus ivory cut in thin strips. The sleds were built short, broad and low. This prevented many a spill, for as Johnny soon learned, the reindeer is a cross between a burro and an ox in his disposition, and, once he has scented a rich bed of mosses and lichens, on which he feeds, he takes on the strength and speed of an ox stampeding for a water hole in the desert, and the stubbornness of a burro drawn away from his favorite thistle.

The deer were driven by a single leather strap; the old, old jerk strap of the days of ox teams. Johnny had demanded at once the privilege of driving but he had made a sorry mess of it. He had jerked the strap to make the deer go more slowly. This really being the signal for greater speed, the deer had bolted across the tundra, at last spilling Johnny and his load of Chukche plunder over a cutbank. This procedure did not please the Chukches, and Johnny was not given a second opportunity to drive. He was compelled to trot along beside the sleds or, back to back with one of his fellow travelers, to ride over the gleaming whiteness that lay everywhere.

It was at such times as these that Johnny had ample opportunity to study the country through which they passed. Lighted as it was by a glorious moon, it presented a grand and fascinating panorama. To the right lay the frozen ocean, its white expanse cut here and there by a pool of salt water pitchy black by contrast with the ice. To the left lay the mountains extending as far as the eye could see, with their dark purple shadows and triangles of light and seeming but another sea, that tempest-tossed and terrible had been congealed by the bitter northern blasts.

When twelve hours of travel had been accomplished, and it had been proposed that they camp for the night, Johnny had been quite free to offer his assistance in setting up the tents. In this he had been even less successful than in his perform-ance with the reindeer. He had set the igloo poles wrong end up and, when these had been righted, had spread the long haired deerskin robes, which were to serve as the inner lining of the shelters, hair side out, which was also wrong. He had once more been relegated to the background. This time he had not cared, for it gave him an opportunity to study his fellow travelers. They were for the most part a dark and sullen bunch. Not understanding Johnny's language, they did not attempt to talk with him, but certain gloomy glances seemed to tell him that, though his money had been accepted by them, there was still some secret reason why he might have been traveling in safer company.

This, however, was more a feeling than an idea based on any overt act of the natives, and Johnny tried to shake it off. That he might do this more quickly, he gave himself over to the study of these strange nomads. Their dress was a one-piece suit made of short haired deer skins. Men, women and children dressed alike, with the exception that very small children were sewed into their garments, hands, feet and all and were strapped on the sleds like bundles.

The food was strange to the American. One needed a good appetite to enjoy it. Great twenty-five pound white fish were produced from skin bags and sliced off to be eaten raw. Reindeer meat was stewed in copper kettles. Hard tack was soaked in water and mixed with reindeer suet. Tea from the ever present Russian tea kettle and seal oil from a sewed up seal skin took the place of drink and rel-ish. The tea was good, the seal oil unspeakable, a liquid not even to be smelled of by a white man, let alone tasted.

By the second day Johnny had found himself confining his associations to one person, who, to all appearances, was a fellow passenger, and not a member of the tribe. He had learned to pitch his own igloo and hers. Not five hours before he had hewn away a hard bank of snow and built there a shelf for his bed. When his igloo was completed he had erected a second not many feet away. This was for his fellow passenger. In case anything should happen he felt that he would like to be near her, and she had shown by many little signs that she shared his feelings in this.

"In case something happened," Johnny reflected drowsily. He had a feeling that, sooner or later, something was going to happen. There was something altogether mysterious about the actions of these Chukches, especially one great sullen fellow, who had come skulking about Johnny's igloo just before he had turned in.

These natives were supposed to be trustworthy, but Johnny had his misgivings and was on his guard. They had come in contact with Russians, perhaps also with Orientals, and had learned treachery.

"And yet," thought Johnny, "what could they want from me? I paid them well for my transportation. They sold their reindeer to the American army for a fat price. They would be more than greedy if they wanted more."

Nevertheless, the air of mystery hung about him like a dark cloud. He could not sleep. And not being able to sleep, he meditated.

He had already begun the eternal round of thoughts that will revolve through a fellow's brain at night, when he heard a sound—the soft crush of a skin boot in the snow it seemed. He listened and thought he heard it again, this time more distinctly, as if the person were approaching his igloo. A chill crept up and down his spine. His right hand involuntarily freed itself from the furs and sought the cold hilt of the Russian knife. He had his army automatic, but where there are many ears to hear a shot, a knife is better.

"What an ideal trap for treachery, this igloo! A villain need but creep through tent-flaps, pause for a breath, then stealthily lift the deer skin curtain. A stab or a shot, and all would be ended." These thoughts sped through Johnny's mind.

Scarcely breathing, he waited for other signs of life abroad at that hour of night— a night sixteen hours long. He heard nothing.

Finally, his mind took up again the endless chain of thought. He had arrived safely at Khabarask, the terminus of the Russian line. Here he had remained for three days, half in hiding, until the "Reindeer Special" had completed its loading and had started on its southern journey to the waiting doughboys. During those three days he had made two startling discoveries; the short Russian of the broad shoulders and sharp chin, he of the envelope of diamonds, was in Khabarask. Johnny had seen him in an eating place, and had had an opportunity to study him without being observed. The man, he concluded, although a total stranger in these parts, was a person of consequence, a leader of some sort, accustomed to being obeyed. There seemed a brutal certainty about the way he ordered the servants of the place to do his bidding. There was a constant wrinkle of a frown between his eyes. A man, perhaps without a sense of humor, he would force every issue to the utmost. Once given an idea, he would override all obstacles to carry it through, not stopping at death, or at many deaths. This had been Johnny's mental analysis of the character of the man, and at once he began to half hate and half admire him. He had lost sight of him immediately, and had not discovered him again. Whether the Russian had left town before the native band did, Johnny could not tell. But, if he had moved on, where did he go?

The other shock was similar in character. The woman who had bought furs for the North had also been in Khabarask. Whether she was a Japanese Johnny was not prepared to say, and that in spite of the fact that he had studied her carefully for five days. She might be a Chukche who, through some strange impulse, had been led south to seek culture and education. He doubted that. She might be an Eskimo from Alaska making her way north to cross Behring Strait in the spring. He doubted that also. Finally she might be a Japanese woman, but in that case, what could be the explanation of her presence here, some two hundred miles north of the last vestige of civilization?

Now, not ten feet from the spot where Johnny lay in an igloo assigned for her private use by the natives, that identical girl slept at this moment. Only four hours before, Johnny had bade her good night, after an enjoyable repast of tea, reindeer meat and hard bread prepared by her own hand over a small wood fire. It was she who was his fellow passenger, whose igloo he had erected, close to his own. Yes, there was mystery enough about the whole situation to keep any fellow awake; yet Johnny hated himself for not sleeping. He felt that the time was coming when he would need stored strength.

He had half dosed off when a sound very close at hand, within the walls of canvas he thought, started him again into wakefulness. His arm ready and free for action, he lay still. His breathing well regulated and even, as in sleep, he watched through narrow slit eyes the deer skin curtain rise, and a head appear. The ugly shaved head of a Chukche it was; and in the intruder's hand was a knife.

The knife startled Johnny. He could not believe his eyes. He thought he was seeing double; yet he did not move.

Slowly, silently the arm of the native rose until it hung over Johnny's heart. In a second it would—

In that second something happened. There came a deadly thwack. The native, without a cry, fell backward beyond the curtain. His knife shot outward too, and stuck hilt downward in the snow.

Johnny drew himself slowly from beneath the furs. Lifting the deer skin curtain cautiously, he looked out. Then he chuckled a cold, dry chuckle. His knuckles were bloody, for the only weapon he had used was that truly American weapon, a clenched fist. Johnny, as I have suggested before, was somewhat handy with his "dukes." His left was a bit out of repair just now, but his right was quite all right, as the crumpled heap of a man testified.

Johnny bent over the man and twisted his head about. No, his neck was not broken. Johnny was thankful for that. He hated to see dead people even when they richly deserved to die.

Then he turned to the knife. He started again, as he extricated the hilt from the snow. But there was no time for examining it. His ear caught a stifled cry, a woman's cry. It came, without a doubt, from the igloo of his fellow traveler, the woman. Hastily thrusting his knife in his belt, he threw back the tentflap and crossed the intervening snowpatch in three strides.

He threw back the canvas just in time to seize a second native by the hood of his deer skin parka. He whirled the man completely about, tossed him high in the air, then struck him as he was coming down; struck him in the same place he had hit the other, only harder, very much harder. He did not examine him later for a broken neck, either.

Turning, Johnny saw the woman staring at him. Evidently she had slept in her furs. As she stood there now, she seemed quite equal to the task of caring for herself. There was a muscular sturdiness about her which Johnny had failed to notice before. In her hand gleamed a wicked looking dagger with a twisted blade.

But that she had been caught unawares, there could be no question, and from the kindly flash in her eyes Johnny read the fact that she was grateful for her deliverance.

He threw one glance at the other igloos. Standing there casting dark, purple shadows, they were strangely silent. Apparently these two murderers had been appointed to accomplish the task alone. The others were asleep. For this Johnny was thankful.

Turning to the woman he said sharply:

"Gotta git outa here. You, me, savvy?"

"Savvy," she replied placidly.

Seizing her fur bag of small belongings, Johnny hastened before her to where the sled deer were tethered. Two sleds were still loaded, one with an unused igloo and deerskins, the other with food. To each of these Johnny hastily harnessed a reindeer. Then whipping out his knife, he cut the tether of all the other deer. They would follow; it was the way of reindeer.

Johnny smiled. These extra deer would spell the others and quicken travel. In case of need, they could be killed for food. Besides, if they had no deer, the treacherous natives could not follow. They would be obliged to return to the Russian town they had left and make a new start, and by that time—Johnny patted his chest where reposed the bill with the Alaskan stamp on it, and murmured:

"Stay with me li'l' ol' one-spot, and I'll take you home."

He cast one more glance toward the igloos. Not a soul had stirred.

"We're off," he exclaimed, leaping on his sled and slapping his reindeer on the thigh with the jerkstrap.

"Yes," the Jap girl smiled as she followed his example.

Johnny thought they were "off," but it took only an instant to tell that they were not. His deer cut a circle and sent him gliding away over the snows. Fortunately he held to his jerkstrap and at last succeeded in stopping the animal's mad rush.

The Jap girl smiled again as she took the jerkstrap from his hand and tied it down short to her own sled. Then she leaped upon her sled again and, with some cooing words spoke to her reindeer. The deer tossed his antlers and trotted quietly away, leaving Johnny to spring upon his own sled and ride in increasing wonderment over the long glistening miles.

When they had traveled for eight hours without a pause and without a balk, the Jap girl allowed her deer to stop. She loosened the draw strap and, turning the animal about, tied him by a long line to the sled, that he might paw moss from beneath the snow in a wide circle.

"How—how'd you know how to drive?" Johnny stammered.

"Never before so," she smiled.

"You mean you never drove a reindeer?"

"Before now, no. Hungry you?" The Jap girl smiled, as if to say, "Enough about that, let's eat."

It was a royal meal they ate together, those two there beneath the Arctic moon. This Jap girl was a wonder, Johnny felt that, and he was to learn it more certainly as the days passed.

Three days later he sat upon a robe of deer skin. The corners of the robe were drawn up over his shoulders. A shelter of deer skins and walrus skins, hastily improvised by him during the beginning of a terrible blizzard which came howling down from the north, was ample to keep the wind from driving the biting snow into their faces, but it could hardly keep out the cold. In spite of that, the Jap girl, buried in deer skins, with her back against his, was sleeping soundly. Johnny was sleeping bolt upright with one ear awake. His reindeer were picketed close to the improvised igloo. Other nights, they had taken turns watching to protect them from prowling wolves, but this night no one could long withstand the numbing cold of the blizzard. So he watched and half slept. Now he caught the rising howl of the wind, and now felt its lull as the deer skins sagged. But what was this? Was there a different note, a howl that was not of the wind?

Shaking himself into entire wakefulness, Johnny sat bolt upright and listened intently. Yes, there it was again. A wolf beyond doubt, as yet some distance away, but coming toward them with the wind.

A wolf, a single one, was not all menace. If he could be shot before his fangs tore at the flesh of a reindeer, there would be gain. He would be food, and at the present moment there was no food. The Jap girl did not know it, but Johnny did. Not a fish, not a hunk of venison, not a pilot biscuit was on their sled. They would soon be reduced to the necessity of killing and eating one of their deer, unless, unless—the howl came more plainly and strangely enough with it came the crack crack of hoofs.

Johnny sprang to his feet. What could that crack cracking of hoofs mean? Had one of his deer already broken his tether?

With automatic in hand, he was out in the storm in an instant. Even as he became accustomed to the dim light, he saw a skulking form drifting down with the wind. Dropping upon his stomach, he took deliberate aim and fired. There was a howl of agony but still the creature came on. Another shot and it turned over tearing at the whirling snow.

Johnny jumped to his feet. "Eats," he murmured.

But then there came that other sound again, the crack crack of hoofs. He peered through the swirling snow, counting his reindeer. They were all there. Here was a mystery. It was not long in solving. He had but to glance to the south of his reindeer to detect some dark object bulking large in the night.

"A deer!" he muttered. "A wild reindeer! What luck!"

It was true. The wolf had doubtless been stalking him. Creeping stealthily forward, foot by foot, Johnny was at last within easy range of the creature. His automatic cracked twice in quick succession and a moment later he was exulting over two hundred pounds of fresh meat, food for many days.

Twenty hours later, Johnny found himself sitting sleepily on the edge of one of the deer sleds. The reindeer, unhitched and tethered, were digging beneath the snow for moss. The storm had subsided and once more they had journeyed far. The Jap girl was buried deep beneath the furs on the other sled.

Johnny was puzzling his brain at this time over one thing. They had followed a half covered, ancient trail due north for two days. Then a fresh track had joined the old one. It was the track of a man with dog team and sled. This they had followed due north again, and two hours ago, while the deer were resting and feeding, Johnny had detected the Jap girl in the act of measuring the footprints of the man who drove the dog team.

She had appeared troubled and embarrassed when she knew that he had seen what she was doing. Notwithstanding the fact that there had been no sign of guilt or treachery in her frank brown eyes, Johnny had been perplexed. What secret was she hiding from him? What did she know, or seek to know, about this man whose trail had joined theirs at an angle? Could it be? No, Johnny dismissed the thought which came to his mind.

He had dismissed all his perplexities, and was about to abandon himself to three winks of sleep, when something on the horizon attracted his attention. A mere dot at first, it grew rapidly larger.

"Dog team or reindeer on our trail," he thought. "I wonder."

From beneath his parka he drew his long blue automatic. After examining its clip, he laid it down on the sled with two other clips beside it. Then he drew the two knives also from his belt; the one he had secured at the time of the street fight in Vladivostok, the other had belonged to the Chukche who had attacked him. For the twentieth time he noted that they were exactly alike, blade forging, hilt carving, and all. And again, this realization set him to speculating. How had this brace of knives got so widely separated? How had this one found its way to the heart of a Chukche tribe? Why had the Chukches attempted to murder the Japanese girl and himself? Had it been with the hope of securing wealth from their simple luggage, or had they been bribed to do it? Once more his brain was in a whirl.

But there was business at hand. The black spot had developed into a reindeer, driven by a man. How many were following this man Johnny could not tell.

CHAPTER IV

A NARROW ESCAPE

As Johnny stood awaiting the arrival of the stranger, many wild misgivings raced through his mind. What if this man was but the forerunner of the whole Chukche tribe? Then indeed, for himself and the Japanese girl things were at an end.

The newcomer was armed with a rifle. Johnny would stand little show with him in a duel, good as his automatic was.

But the man came on with a jaunty swing that somehow was reassuring. Who could he be? As he came close, he dropped his rifle on his sled and approached with empty hands.

"I am Iyok-ok," he said in good English, at the same time thrusting out his hand. "I was an American soldier, an Eskimo. Now I am going back to my home at Cape Prince of Wales."

"You got your discharge easily," smiled Johnny.

"Not so easy, but I got it."

"Well, anyway, stranger," said Johnny gripping the other's hand, "I can give you welcome, comrade. We are traveling the same way."

The Eskimo looked at Johnny's regulation army shoes as he said the word comrade, but made no comment.

"Know anything about travel in such a country?" asked Johnny.

"Most things you need to know."

"Then you sure are welcome," Johnny declared. Then, as he looked at the Eskimo closely there came to him a feeling that they had met before but where and when he could not recall. He did not mention the fact, but merely motioned the stranger to a seat on the sled while he dug into his pack for a morsel of good cheer.

Many days later, Johnny lay sprawled upon a double thickness of long haired deer skins. He was reading a book. Two seal oil lamps sputtered in the igloo, but these were for heat, not for light. Johnny got his light in the form of a raggedly round patch of sunlight which fell straight down from the top where the poles of the igloo met.

Johnny was very comfortable physically, but not entirely at ease mentally. He had been puzzled by something that had happened five minutes before. Moreover, he was half angry at his enforced idleness here.

Yet he was very comfortable. The igloo was a permanent one. Erected at the base of a cliff, covered over with walrus skin, lined with deer skin, and floored with planks hewn from driftwood logs, it was perfect for a dwelling of its kind. It stood in a hunting village on the Siberian shore of Behring Sea. The Jap girl, Johnny and Iyok-ok had traveled thus far in safety.

Yes, they had come a long distance, many hundreds of miles. As Johnny thought of it now, he put his book aside (a dry, old novel, left here by some American seaman) and dreamed those days all through again.

Wonderful days had followed the addition of Iyok-ok to their party. From that hour they had wanted nothing of food or shelter. Reared as he apparently had been in such wilds as these, the native skillfully had sought out the best of game, the driest, most sheltered of camping spots, in fact, had done everything that tended to make life easy in such a land.

Johnny's reveries were cut short and he started suddenly to his feet. A pebble had dropped squarely upon the deer skin spread out before him. It had come through the hole in the peak of the igloo. He glanced quickly up, but saw nothing.

Then he grinned. "Just a case of nerves, I guess. Some kids playing on the cliff. Anyway, I'll investigate," he said to himself.

Throwing back the deerskin flap, he stepped outside. Did he see a boot disappear around the point of the cliff above the igloo? He could not tell. At any rate, there was no use wasting more time on the question. To see farther around the cliff, one must climb up its rough face, and by that time any mischief maker might have disappeared.

Yet Johnny stood there worried and puzzled. Twice in the last hour pebbles had rattled down upon the igloo, and now one had dropped inside. An old grievance stirred him: Why were not he and his strange companions on their way? With only four hundred miles to travel to East Cape, with a splendid trail, with reindeer well fed and rested, it seemed folly to linger in this native village. The reindeer Chukches, whose sled deer they had borrowed, might be upon them at any moment, and that, Johnny felt sure, would result in an unpleasant mixup. Yet he had been utterly unable to get the little Oriental girl and Iyok-ok to go on. Why? He could only guess. There were a great many other things he could only guess at. The little Oriental girl's reason for going so far into the wilderness was as much a secret as ever. He could only guess that it had to do with the following of that mysterious driver of a dog team. With unerring precision this man had pushed straight on northward toward East Cape and Behring Strait. And they had followed, not, so far as Johnny was concerned, because they were interested in him, but because he had traveled their way.

At times they had come upon his camp. Located at the edge of some bank or beside some willow clump, where there was shelter from the wind, these camps told little or nothing of the man who had made them. Everything which might tell tales had been carried on or burned. Once only Johnny had found a scrap of paper. Nothing had been written on it. From it Johnny had learned one thing only: it had originally come from some Russian town, for it had the texture of Russian bond. But this was little news.

Who was this stranger who traveled so far? Johnny had a feeling that he was at the moment hiding in this native village, and that this was the reason his two companions did not wish to proceed. There had grown up between these two, the Eskimo boy and the Japanese girl, a strange friendship. At times Johnny had suspicions that this friendship had existed before they had met on the tundra. However that might have been, they seemed now to be working in unison. Only the day before he had happened to overhear them conversing in low tones, and the language, he would have sworn, was neither Eskimo, English, nor Pidgen. Yet he did not question the boy's statement that he was an American Eskimo. Indeed there were times when the flash of his honest smile made Johnny believe that they had met somewhere in America. On his trip to Nome and Fairbanks before the war, Johnny had met many Eskimos, and had boxed and wrestled with some of the best of them.

"Oh, well," he sighed, and stretched himself, "'tain't that I've got a string on 'em, nor them on me. I'll have to wait or go on alone, that's all."

He entered the igloo, and tried again to become interested in his book, but his mind kept returning to the strange friendship which had grown up between the three of them, Iyok-ok, the Jap girl and himself. The Jap girl had proved a good sport indeed. She might have ridden all the time, but she walked as far in a day as they did. She cooked their meals cheerfully, and laughed over every mishap.

So they had traveled northward. Three happy children in a great white wilderness, they pitched their igloos at night, a small one for the girl, a larger one for the two men, and, burying themselves beneath the deer skins, had slept the dreamless sleep of children, wearied from play.

The Jap girl had appeared to be quite content to be going into an unknown wilderness. Only once she had seemed concerned. That was when a long detour had taken them from the track of the unknown traveler, but her cheerfulness had returned once they had come upon his track again. This had set Johnny speculating once more. Who was this stranger? Was he related to the girl in some way? Was he her friend or her foe? Was he really in this village at this time? If so, why did she not seek him out? If a friend, why did she not join him; and, if an enemy, why not have him killed? Surely, here they were quite beyond the law.

Oh, yes, Johnny might get a dog team and go on up the coast alone, but Johnny liked his two traveling companions too well for that, and besides, Johnny dearly loved mysteries, and here was a whole nest of them. No, Johnny would wait.

The seal oil lamps imparted a drowsy warmth to the igloo. The deer skins were soft and comfortable. Johnny grew sleepy. Throwing the ragged old book in the corner, he stretched out full length on the skins, which lay in the irregular circle of light, and was soon fast asleep.

Just how long he slept he could not tell. When he awoke it was with a feeling of great peril tugging at his heart. His first conscious thought was that the aperture above him had, in some way, been darkened. Instantly his eyes sought that opening. What he saw there caused his heart to pause and his eyes to bulge.

Directly above him, seemingly poised for a drop, was a vicious looking hook. With a keen point and a barb fully three inches across, with a shaft of half-inch steel which was driven into a pole three inches in diameter and of indefinite length, it could drive right through Johnny's stomach, and pin him to the planks beneath. And, as his startled eyes stared fixedly at it, the thing shot downward.

CHAPTER V

"FRIEND? ENEMY?"

Johnny Thompson, before he joined the army, had been considered one of the speediest men of the boxing ring. His brain worked like lightning, and every muscle in his body responded instantly to its call. Johnny had not lost any of his speed. It was well that he had not, for, like a spinning car-wheel, he rolled over twice before the hook buried itself to the end of its barb in the pungent plank on which he had reclined an instant before.

Nor did Johnny stop rolling then. He continued until he bumped against the skin wall of his abode. This was fortunate also, for he had not half regained his senses when two almost instantaneous explosions shook the igloo, tore the plank floor into shreds, shooting splinters about, and even through the double skin wall, and filling Johnny's eyes with powder smoke and dust.

Johnny sat up with one hand on his automatic. He was fully awake.

"Is that all?" he drawled. "Thanks! It's enough, I should say. Johnny Thompson exit." A wry grin was on his face. "Johnny Thompson killed by a falling whale harpoon; shot to death by a whale gun; blown to atoms by a whale bomb. Exit Johnny. They do it in the movies, I say!"

But that was not quite all. The blazing seal oil lamps had overturned. Splinters from the floor were catching fire. Johnny busied himself at beating these out. As soon as this had been accomplished, he stepped outside.

From an awe-struck ring of native women and children, who had been attracted by the explosion, the little Jap girl darted.

"Oh, Meester Thompsie!" she exclaimed, wringing her hands, "so terrible, awful a catastrophe! Are you not killed? So terrible!"

Johnny grinned.

"Nope," he said, putting out a hand to console her. "I'm not killed, nor even blown to pieces. What I'd like to know is, who dropped that harpoon."

He looked from face to face of the silent circle. Not one showed a sign of any knowledge of the affair. They had heard the explosion and had run from their homes to see what had happened.

Turning toward the cliff, from which the harpoon had been dropped, Johnny studied it carefully. No trace of living creature was to be discovered there. Then he looked again at the circle of brown faces, seeking any recent arrival. There was none.

"Come!" he said to the Jap girl.

Taking her hand, he led her from house to house of the village. Beyond two to three old women, too badly crippled to walk, the houses were found to contain no one.

"Well, one thing is sure," Johnny observed, "the Chukche reindeer herders have not come. It was not they who did it."

"No," answered the Jap girl.

"Say!" exclaimed Johnny, in a tone more severe than he had ever used with his companion, "why in thunder can't we get out of this hole? What are we sticking here for?"

"Can't tell." The girl wrung her hands again. "Can't tell. Can't go, that's all. You go; all right, mebby. Can't go my. That's all. Mebby go to-morrow; mebby next day. Can't tell."

Johnny was half inclined to believe that she was in league with the treachery which hung over the place, and had shown itself in the form of loaded harpoons, but when he realized that she did not urge him to stay, he found it impossible to suspect her.

"Well, anyway, darn it!"

"What?" she smiled.

"Oh, nothing," he growled, and turned away.

Two hours later Johnny was lying on the flat ledge of the rocky cliff from which the harpoon had been dropped. He was, however, a hundred feet or more down toward the bay. He was watching a certain igloo, and at the same time keeping an eye on the shore ice. Iyok-ok had gone seal hunting. When he returned over the ice, Johnny meant to have a final confab with him in regard to starting north.

As to the vigil he kept on the igloo, that was the result of certain suspicions regarding the occupants of that particular shelter. There was a dog team which hung about the place. These dogs were larger and sleeker than the other animals of the village. Their fights with other dogs were more frequent and severe. That would naturally mark them as strangers. Johnny had made several journeys of a mile or two up and down the beach trail, and, as far as he could tell, the man of mystery whose trail they had followed to this village had not left the place.

"Of course," he had told himself, "he might have been one of the villagers returning to his home. But that doesn't seem probable."

From all this, Johnny had arrived at the conclusion that the watching of this house would yield interesting results.

It did. He had not been lying on the cliff half an hour, when the figure of a man came backing out of the igloo's entrance. Johnny whistled. He was sure he had seen that pair of shoulders before. And the parka the man wore; it was not of the very far north. There was a smoothness about the tan and something about the cut of it that marked it at once as coming from a Russian shop, such as Wo Cheng kept.

"And squirrel skin!" Johnny breathed.

He was not kept long in doubt as to the identity of the wearer. As the man turned to look behind him, Johnny saw the sharp chin of the Russian, the man of the street fight and the many diamonds. He had acquired something of a beard, but there was no mistaking those frowning brows, square shoulders and that chin.

"So," Johnny thought, "he is the fellow we have been trailing. The Jap girl wanted to follow him and so, perhaps, did Iyok-ok. I wonder why? And say, old dear," he whispered, "I wonder if it could have been you who dropped that harpoon. It's plain enough from the looks of you that you'd do it, once you fancied you'd half a reason. I've a good mind—" His hand reached for his automatic.

"No," he decided, "I won't do it. I don't really know that you deserve it; besides I hate corpses, and things like that. But I say!"

A new and wonderful thought had come to him. He felt that, at any rate, he owed this person something, and he should have it. Beside Johnny on the ledge, where some native had left it, out of reach of the dog's, was a sewed up seal skin full of seal oil. To the native of the north seal oil is what Limburger cheese is to a Dutchman. He puts it away in skin sacks to bask in the sun for a year or more and ripen. This particular sackful was "ripe"; it was over ripe and had been for some time. Johnny could tell that by the smooth, balloon-like rotundity of the thing. In fact, he guessed it was about due to burst. Once Johnny had taken a cup of this liquid for tea. He had it close enough to his face to catch a whiff of it. He could still recall the smell of it.

Now his right hand smoothed the bloated skin tenderly. He twisted it about, and balanced it in his hand. Yes, he could do it! The Russian was not looking up. There was a convenient ledge, some three feet above his head. There the sack would strike and burst. The boy smiled, in contemplation of that bursting.

"This for what you may have done," Johnny whispered, and balancing the sack in his hand, as if it had been a football, he gave it a little toss. Over the cliff it went to a sheer fall of fifteen feet. There followed a muffled explosion. It had burst! Johnny saw the Russian completely deluged with the vile smelling liquid. Then he ducked.

As he lay flat on the ledge, he caught a silvery laugh. Looking quickly about, he found himself staring into the eyes of the little Jap girl. She had been watching him.

"You—you—know him?" he stammered.

The girl shrugged her shoulders.

"Your friend?"

She shook her head vigorously.

"Enemy? Kill?" Johnny's hand sought his automatic.

"No! No! No!" she fairly screamed. "Not kill!" Her hand was on his arm with a frantic grip.

"Why?"

"No can tell. Only, not kill; not kill now. No! No! No! Mebby never!"

"Well, I'll be—" Johnny took his hand from his gun and peered over the ledge. The man was gone. It was a dirty trick he had played. He half wished he had not done it. And yet, the Jap girl had laughed. She knew what the man was. She had been close enough to have stopped him, had she thought it right. She had not done so. His conscience was clear.

They crept away in the gathering darkness, these two; and Johnny suddenly felt for this little Jap girl a comradeship that he had not known before. It was such a feeling as he had experienced in school days, when he was prowling about with boy pals.

Shortly after darkness had fallen, Johnny was seated cross-legged on a deer skin, staring gloomily at the ragged hole left by the whale harpoon bomb. He had not yet seen Iyok-ok. He was trying now to unravel some of the mysteries which the happenings of the day had served only to tangle more terribly. He had not meant to kill the Russian, even though the Jap girl had told him to; Johnny did not kill people, unless it was in defense of his country or his life. He had been merely trying the Jap girl out. He was obliged to admit now that he had got nowhere. She had laughed when he had played that abominable trick on the Russian; had denied that the stranger was her friend, yet had at once become greatly excited when Johnny proposed to kill him. What could a fellow make of all this? Who was this Jap girl anyway, and why had she followed this Russian so far? Somehow, Johnny could not help but feel that the Russian was a deep dyed plotter of some sort. He was inclined to believe that he had had much to do with that harpoon episode as well as the murder attempted by the reindeer Chukches.

"By Jove!" the American boy suddenly slapped his knee. "The knife, the two knives exactly alike. One he tried to use in the street fight at Vladivostok; the other he must have given to the reindeer Chukche to use on anyone who might follow him."

For a time he sat in deep thought. As he weighed the probabilities for and against this theory, he found himself doubting. There might be many knives of this pattern. The knife might have been stolen from him by the Chukche, or the Russian might have given it to the native as a reward for service, having no idea to what deadly purposes it would be put. And, again, if he were that type of plotter, would not the Jap girl know of it, and desire him killed?

The Japanese girl puzzled Johnny more and more. Her friendship for Iyok-ok, her eagerness to protect the Russian—what was to be made of all this? Were the three of them, after all, leagued together in deeds of darkness? And was he, Johnny, a pawn to be sacrificed at the proper moment?

And the Russian, why was he traveling so far north? What possible interests could he have here? Was he, too, planning to cross the Strait to America? Or was he in search of wealth hidden away in this frozen land?

"The furs! I'll bet that's it!" Johnny slapped his knee. "This Russian has come north to demand tribute for his government from the hunting Chukches. They're rich in furs—mink, ermine, red, white, silver gray and black fox. A man could carry a fortune in them on one sled. Yes, sir! That's his business up here."

But then, the diamonds? Again Johnny seemed to have reached the end of a blind alley in his thinking. Who could be so rash as to carry thousands of dollars' worth of jewels on such a trip? And yet, he was not certain the man had them now. He had seen them but once, and that in the disguise shop.

Further thoughts were cut short by a head thrust in at the flap of the igloo. It was Iyok-ok.

"Go soon," he smiled. "Mebby two hours."

"North?"

"Eh-eh" (yes), he answered, lapsing into Eskimo.

"All right."

The head disappeared.

"Well, anyway, my seal oil bath did some good," Johnny remarked to himself. "It jarred the old fox out of his lair and started him on his way."

He wondered a little about the Jap girl. Would she still travel with them? These musings were cut short when he carried his bundle to the deer sled. She was there to greet him with a broad smile. And so once more they sped away over the tundra in the moonlight.

They had not gone five miles before Johnny had assured himself that once more the Russian and his dog team had preceded them.

CHAPTER VI

"NOW I SHALL KILL YOU"

Johnny Thompson was at peace with the world. He was engaged in the most delightful of all occupations, gathering gold. He had often dreamed of gathering gold. He had dreamed, too, of finding money strewn upon the street. But now, here he was, with one of these choice Russian knives, picking away at clumps of frozen earth and picking up, as they fell out, particles of gold. Some were tiny; many were large as a pea, and one had been the size of a hickory nut. Now and again he straightened up to swing a pick into the frozen gravel which lay within the circle of light made by his pocket flashlight. After a few strokes he would throw down the pick and begin breaking up the lumps. Every now and again, he would lift the small sack into which the lumps were dropped. It grew heavier every moment.

It was quite dark all about him; indeed, Johnny was nearly a hundred feet straight into the heart of a cut bank, and, to start on this straight ahead drift, he had been obliged to lower himself into a shaft as into a well, a drop of fifteen feet or more. That the mine had other drifts he knew, but this one suited him. That it had another occupant he also knew, but this did not trouble him. He was too much interested in the yellow glitter of real gold to think of danger. And he was half dazed by the realization that there could be a gold mine like this in Siberia. Alaska had gold, plenty of it, of course, and he was now less than two hundred miles from Alaska, but he had never dreamed that the dreary slopes of the Kamchatkan Peninsula could harbor such wealth. Someone had been mining it, too, but that must have been months, perhaps years, ago. The pick handles were rough with decay, the pans red with rust.

Curiosity had led Johnny to this spot, a half mile from the native village at the mouth of the Anadir River. He had been marooned again in that village. They had covered three hundred miles on their last journey, then had come another pause. This time, though he did not even see his dogs about the village, Johnny felt sure that the Russian had once more taken to hiding.

Having nothing else to do, Johnny had followed a narrow track up the river. The track had come to an end at the entrance to the mine. Thinking it merely a sort of crude cold storage plant for keeping meat fresh, he had let himself down to explore it. Increasing curiosity had led him on until he had discovered the gold. Now he had quite forgotten the person whose tracks led him to the spot.

He was shocked into instant and vivid realization of peril by a cold pressure on his temple and a voice which said in the preciseness of a foreigner:

"Now I have you, sir. Now I shall kill you, sir."

In that instant Johnny prepared himself for his final earthly sensation. He had recognized the voice of the Russian.

There came a click, then a snap. The next instant the revolver which had rested against his forehead struck the frozen roof of the mine. The weapon had missed fire and, between turns of the cylinder, Johnny's good right hand had struck out and up.

The light snapped out, and in the midnight darkness of that icy cavern the two grappled and fell.

Had Johnny been in possession of the full power of his left arm, the battle would have been over soon. As it was they rolled over and over, their bodies crushing frozen bits of pay-dirt, like twin rollers. They struggled for mastery. Each man realized that, unless some unforeseen power intervened, defeat meant death. The Russian fought with the stubbornness of his race; fought unfairly too, biting and kicking when opportunity permitted. Three times Johnny barely missed a blow on the head which meant unconsciousness, then death.

At last, panting, perspiring, bleeding and bruised, Johnny clamped his right arm about his antagonist's neck and, flopping his body across his chest, lay there until the Russian's muscles relaxed.

Sliding to a sitting position, the American began feeling about in the dark. At last, gripping a flashlight, he snapped it on. The face of the Russian revealed the fact that he was not unconscious. Johnny slid to a position which brought each knee down upon one of the Russian's arms. He would take no chances with that man.

Slowly Johnny flashed the light about, then, with a little exclamation, he reached out and gripped the handle of the Russian's revolver.

"Now," he mocked, "now I have you, sir. Now I shall kill you, sir."

He had hardly spoken the words when a body hurled itself upon him, knocking the revolver from his hand and extinguishing the light.

"So. There are others! Let them come," roared Johnny, striking out with his right in the dark.

"Azeezruk nucky." To his astonishment he recognized the voice of Iyok-ok. What he had said, in Eskimo, was, "It would be a bad thing to kill him," meaning doubtless the Russian.

"Azeezruk adocema" (he is a bad one), replied Johnny, throwing the light on the sullen face of the Eskimo.

"Eh-eh" (yes), the other agreed.

"Then what in thunder!" Johnny exclaimed, falling back on English. "He tried to kill me. Kill me! Do you understand? Why shouldn't I kill him?"

"No kill," said the Eskimo stubbornly.

Johnny sat and thought for a full three minutes. In that time, his blood had cooled. He was able to reason about the matter. In the army he had learned one rule: "If someone knows more about a matter than you do, follow his guidance, though, at the time, it seems dead wrong." Evidently Iyok-ok knew more about this Russian than Johnny did. Then the thing to do was to let the man go.

Before releasing him, he searched him carefully. Beyond a few uninteresting papers, a pencil, a cigaret case and a purse he found nothing. Evidently the revolver had been his only weapon.

As he searched the man, one peculiar question flashed through Johnny's mind; if the Russian had the envelope full of diamonds on his person, what should he do, take them or leave them? He was saved the necessity of a decision; they were not there.

"Now," said Johnny, seating himself on a rusty pan, as the Russian went shuffling out of the mine, "tell me why you didn't let me kill him."

"Can't tell," was Iyok-ok's laconic reply.

"Why?"

"Not now. Sometime, maybe. Not now."

"Look here," said Johnny savagely, "that man has tried to kill me or have me killed, three times, is it not so?"

Iyok-ok did not answer.

"First," Johnny went on, "he induces the reindeer Chukches to try to kill me and furnishes them the knife to do it with. Eh?"

"Maybe."

"Second, he drops a harpoon into my igloo and tries to harpoon me and blow me up."

"Maybe."

"And now he puts a revolver to my head and pulls the trigger. Still you say 'No kill.' What shall I make of that?"

"Canak-ti-ma-na" (I don't know), said the Eskimo. "No kill, that's all."

Johnny was too much astonished and perplexed to say anything further. The two sat there for some time in silence. At last the Eskimo rose and made his way toward the entrance.

Johnny flashed his light about the place. He was looking for his sack of gold. Suddenly he uttered an exclamation and put out his hand. What it grasped was the envelope he had seen in the Russian's pocket at Wo Cheng's shop, the envelope of diamonds. And the diamonds were still there; he could tell that by the feel of the envelope.

Hastily searching out his now insignificant treasure of gold, Johnny placed it with the envelope of diamonds in his inner pocket and hurried from the mine.

Darkness again found him musing over a seal oil lamp. He was not in a very happy mood. He was weary of orientalism and mystery. He longed for the quiet of his little old town, Chicago. Wouldn't it be great to put his feet under his old job and say, "Well, Boss, what's the dope to-day?" Wouldn't it, though? And to go home at night to doll up in his glad rags and call on Mazie. Oh, boy! It fairly made him sick to think of it.

But, at last, his mind wandered back to the many mysteries which had been straightened out not one bit by these events of the day. Here he was traveling with two companions, a Jap girl and an Eskimo. Eskimo? Right there he began to wonder if Iyok-ok, as he called himself, was really an Eskimo after all. What if he should turn out to be a Jap playing the part of an Eskimo? Only that day Johnny had once more come upon him suddenly to find him in earnest conversation with the Jap girl. And the language they had been using had sounded distinctly oriental. And yet, if he was a Jap, how did it come about that he spoke the Eskimo language so well?

Dismissing this question, his mind dwelt upon the events of the past few days. Twice he had been begged not to kill the Russian. This last time he most decidedly would have been justified in putting a bullet into the rascal's brain. He had been prevented from doing so by Iyok-ok. Why?

"Anyway," he said to himself, yawning, "I'm glad I didn't do it. It's nasty business, this killing people. I couldn't very well tell such a thing to Mazie; you can't tell such things to a woman, and I want to tell her all about things over here. It's been a hard old life, but so far I haven't done a single thing that I wouldn't be proud to tell her about. No, sir, not one! I can say: 'Mazie, I did this and I did that,' and Mazie'll say, 'Oh, Johnny! Wasn't that gr-ran-nd?'"

Johnny grinned as the thought of it and felt decidedly better. After all, what was the use of living if one was to live on and on and on and never have any adventures worth the telling?

For some time he lay sprawled out before the lamp in silent reflection, then he sat up suddenly and pounded his knee.

"By Jove! I'll bet that's it!" he exclaimed.

He had happened upon a new theory regarding the Russian. It seemed probable to him that this man, knowing of this gold mine, perhaps being owner of it, had come north to determine its value and the advisability of opening it for operation in the spring. In these days, when the money market of the world was gold hungry, that glittering, yellow metal was of vast importance, especially to the warring factions of Russia. Surely, this seemed a plausible explanation. And if it was true then he could hurry on up the coast, with or without his companions and make his way home.

"But then," he said, perplexed again. He reached his hand into his pocket to draw out the envelope he had found in the mine. "But then, there's the diamonds. Would a man coming on such a journey bring such treasure with him? He couldn't trade them to the natives. They know money well enough, but not diamonds."

Johnny opened the envelope and shook it gently. Three stones fell into his hand. They were of purest blue white, perfect stones and perfectly cut. A glance at the envelope showed him that it was divided into four narrow compartments and that each compartment was filled with diamonds wrapped in tissue paper. Only these three were unwrapped.

Running his fingers down the outside of the compartments, he counted the jewels.

"One hundred and four," he breathed. "A king's ransom. Forty or fifty thousand dollars worth, anyway. Whew!"

Then he stared and his hand shook. His eye had fallen upon the stamp of the seal in the corner of the envelope. He knew that secret mark all too well; had learned it from Wo Cheng. It was the stamp of the biggest and worst society of Radicals in all the world.

"So!" Johnny whispered to himself. "So, Mr. Russian, you are a Radical, a red, a Nihilist, a communist, an anything-but-society-as-it-is guy. You want the world to cough up its dough and own nothing, and yet here you are carrying round the price of a farm in your vest pocket." He chuckled. "Some reformer, I'd say!"

But his next thought sobered him. What was he to do with all that wealth? One of those stones would make Mazie happy for a lifetime. But it wasn't his. He had no right to it. He could not do a thing he'd be ashamed to tell Mazie and his old boss about.

But, if they didn't belong to him, perhaps the diamonds didn't belong to the Russian either. At any rate, the latter's disloyalty to his nation had forfeited his right to own property.

Even should this Russian be the rightful owner, Johnny could not very well hunt him up and say: "Here, mister. You tried to kill me yesterday. Here are your diamonds. I found them in the mine. Please count them and see if they are all there."

Johnny grinned as he thought of that. There seemed to be nothing to do but keep the stones, for the time being at least.

"Anyway," he said to himself as he rolled up in his deer skins. "I'll bet I have discovered something. I'll bet he's one of the big ones, perhaps the biggest of them all. And he's trying to make his way across to America to stir things up over there."

CHAPTER VII

SAVED FROM THE MOB

"What do you know about that gold mine?" Johnny asked, turning an inquiring eye on Iyok-ok, whom Johnny now strongly suspected of being a Japanese and a member of the Mikado's secret service as well.

"Which mine?" Iyok-ok smiled good-naturedly as he blinked in the sunlight. It was the morning after Johnny's battle with the Russian.

"Are there others?"

"Seven mines."

"Seven! And all of them rich as the one we were in yesterday?"

The boy shrugged his shoulders.

"Some much richer," he declared.

"How long has the world known of this wealth?"

"Never has known. A few men know, that's all. The old Czar, he knew, but would let no one work the mines. Just at the last he said 'Yes.' Then they hurried much machinery over here, but it was too late. The Czar—well, you know he is dead now, but they have their machinery here still."

"Who are 'they'?" asked Johnny with curiosity fully aroused.

"American. I know. Can't tell. Worked for them once. Promise never tell."

Johnny wrinkled his brow but did not press the matter.

"But this Russia, the Kamchatkan Peninsula?" Iyok-ok continued. "Whom does it belong to now? Can you tell me that?"

Johnny shook his head.

"Neither can They tell. If They knew, and if They knew it was safe to come back and mine here, when the world has so great need of gold, you better believe They would come and mine, But They do not know; They do not know." The boy pronounced the last words with an undertone of mystery. "Sometime I will know. Then I—I will tell you, perhaps."

"Where's the machinery?" asked Johnny. "Up the river. Wanta see it?"

"Sure."

They hurried away up the frozen river and in fifteen minutes came upon a row of low sheds. The doors were locked, but to his great surprise Johnny discovered that his companion had the keys.

They were soon walking through dark aisles, on each side of which were piled parts of mining machines of every description, crushers, rollers, smelters and various accessories connected with quartz mining. Mingled with these were picks, pans, steam thawers, windlasses, and great piles of sluice timber. All these last named were for mining placer gold.

"Quartz too?" asked Johnny.

"Plenty of quartz," grinned Iyok-ok. "Come out here, I will show you."

They stepped outside. The boy locked the door, then led his companion up a steep slope until they were on a low point commanding a view of the village below and a rocky cliff above.

"See that cliff?" asked Iyok-ok. "Plenty of gold there. Pick it out with your pen knife. Rich! Too rich."

"Then this Peninsula is as rich as Alaska?"

"Alaska?" Iyok-ok grinned. "Alaska? What shall I say? Alaska, it is a joke. Think of the great Lena River! Great as the Yukon. Who knows what gold is deposited in the beds and banks of that mighty stream? Who knows anything about this wonderful peninsula? The Czar, he has kept it locked. But now the Czar is dead. The key is lost. Who will find it? Sometime we will see."

The boy was interrupted by wild shouts coming from the village. As their eyes turned in that direction, Johnny and Iyok-ok beheld a strange sight. The entire village had apparently turned out to give chase to one man. And, down to the last child, they were armed. But such strange implements of warfare as they carried! All were relics of by-gone days; lances, walrus harpoons, bows and arrows, axes, hammers and many more.

As Johnny watched them, he remembered having been told by an old native that during and after the great war these people had been unable to procure a sufficient supply of ammunition and had been obliged to resort to ancient methods of hunting. These were the bow and arrow, the lance and the harpoon. Powerful bows, of some native wood, shot arrows tipped with cunningly tempered bits of steel. The drawn and tempered barrel of a discarded rifle formed a point for the long-shafted lance. The harpoon, most terrible of all weapons, both for man and beast, was a long wooden shaft with a loose point attached to a long skin rope. Once five or six of these had been thrown into the body of a great white bear or some offending human he was doomed to die a death of agonizing torture; his body being literally torn to pieces by the drag upon the strong skin ropes, fastened to the steel points imbedded in his flesh.

Now it seemed evident that for some misdeed one member of the tribe had been condemned to die. As Johnny stood there staring, the whole affair seemed so much like things he had seen done on the screen, that he found it difficult to realize that this was an actual tragedy, being enacted before his very eyes.

"They do it in the movies," he said.

"Yes," his companion agreed, "but here they will kill him. We must hurry to help him."

"Who is he?"

"Don't you see? The Russian."

"Oh!" sighed Johnny. "Let 'em have him. He deserves as much from me, probably deserves more from them."

"No! No! No!" Iyok-ok protested, now very much excited. "That will never do. We must save him. They think he's from the Russian Government. Think he will demand their furs and carry them away. They mistake. They will kill him. Your automatic! We must hurry. Come."

Johnny found himself being dragged down the hill. As he looked below, he realized that his companion was right. The man was doomed unless they interfered. Already skillful archers were pausing to shoot and their arrows fell dangerously near the fugitive.

"Now, from here," panted Iyok-ok. "Your automatic. Shoot over their heads. They will stop. I will tell them. They will not kill him."

Johnny's hand went to his automatic, but there it rested. These natives? What did he have against them that he should interrupt them in the chase? And this Russian, what claim did he have on him that he should save his life? None, the answer was plain. And yet, here was this boy, to whom he had grown strangely attached, begging him to help save the Russian. A strange state of affairs, for sure.

Toward them, as he ran, the Russian turned a white, appealing face. To them came ever louder and more appalling the cry of the excited natives. Now an arrow fell three feet short of its mark. And now, a stronger arm sent one three yards beyond the man, but a foot to one side. The whole scene, set as it was in the purple shadows and yellow lights of the north-land, was fascinating. But the time had come to act.

"Well, then," Johnny grunted, whipping out his automatic, "for your sake I'll do it."

Three times the automatic barked its vicious challenge. The mob paused and waited silently.

Out of this silence there came a voice. It was the voice of Iyok-ok by Johnny's side. Through cupped hands, he was speaking calmly to the natives. His words were a jumble of Eskimo, Chukche and pidgen-English, but Johnny knew they understood, for, as the speech went on, he saw them drop their weapons, then one by one pick them up again to go shuffling away.

Johnny looked about for the Russian. He had disappeared.

"Now what did you do that for?" he asked his companion.

"Can't tell now," Iyok-ok answered slowly. "Sometime, mebbe. Not now. Azeezruk nucky, that's all."

He paused and looked away at the hills; then turning, extended his hand. "Anyway, I thank you very, very much I thank you."

With that they made their way toward the village and the sea, which, packed and glistening with ice, reflected all the glories of the gorgeous Arctic sunset.

Three hours later Iyok-ok put his head in at Johnny's igloo and said:

"One hour go."

"North?" asked Johnny.

"North."

"You go?"

"Eh-eh."

"Jap girl go?"

"Eh-eh."

"East Cape? Behring Strait?"

"Mebbe." With a smile, the boy was gone.

"Evidently the Russian is on the move again," Johnny observed to himself. "Wonder what he intends to do about his diamonds? Well, anyway, that proves that the gold mines are not his goal."

As Johnny dug into his pack for a dry pair of deer skin stocks, he discovered that his belongings had been tampered with.

"The Russian," he decided, "evidently hasn't forgotten his diamonds."

CHAPTER VIII

WHEN AN ESKIMO BECOMES A JAP

Johnny Thompson smiled as he drew on a pair of rabbit skin trousers, then a parka made of striped ground squirrel skin, finished with a hood of wolf skin. It was not his own suit; it had been borrowed from his host, a husky young hunter of East Cape. But that was not his reason for smiling. He was amused at the thought of the preposterous misunderstanding which his traveling companions had concerning him.

Only the day before he had exclaimed:

"Iyok-ok, I believe I have guessed why the Russian wants to kill me."

"Why?"

"He thinks I am a member of the United States Secret Service."

"Well? Canak-ti-ma-na" (I don't know).

The boy had looked him squarely in the eye as much as to say, "Who could doubt that?"

At first Johnny had been inclined to assure Iyok-ok that there was no truth in the assumption, but the more he thought of it, the better he was satisfied with things as they were. His companions carried with them a great air of mystery; why should he not share this a little with them? He had let the matter drop.

But now, since he was considered to be a member of a secret service organization, he prepared to act the part for one night at least. With the wolf skin parka hood drawn well around his face, he would hardly be recognized, garbed as he was in borrowed clothes.

The mysterious Russian had adopted a plan of sending his dogs to some outpost to be cared for by natives. This made the locating of the igloo he occupied extremely difficult. It had been by the merest chance that Johnny had caught a glimpse of him as he disappeared through the flaps of a dwelling near the center of the village. The American had resolved to watch that place and discover, if possible, some additional clues to the purpose of the Russian.

Skulking from igloo to igloo, Johnny came at last to the one he sought. Making his way to the back of it, he studied it carefully. There were no windows and but one entrance. There was an opening at the top but to climb up there was to be detected. He crept round to the other corner. There a glad sigh escaped his lips. A spot of light shone through the semi-transparent outer covering of walrus skin. That meant that there was a hole in the inner lining of deer skin. He had only to cut a hole through the walrus skin to get a clear view of the interior. This he did quickly and silently.

He swung his arm in disgust as he peered inside. Only an old Chukche woman sat in the corner, chewing and sewing at a skin boot sole.

Johnny hesitated. Had he mistaken the igloo? Had the Russian purposely misled him? He was beginning to think so, when his eye caught the end of a sleeping bag protruding from a pile of deer skins. This he instantly recognized as belonging to the Russian.

"Evidently our friend is out. Then I'll wait," he whispered to himself.

He had been there but a few moments, when the native woman, putting away her work, went out. She had scarcely disappeared through the flap than a dark brown streak shot into the room. As Johnny watched it, he realized that it was a small woman, and, though her clothing was unfamiliar, he knew by certain quick and peculiar movements that this was the Jap girl.

Ah ha! Now, perhaps, he should learn some things. Perhaps after all these three were in league; perhaps they were all Radicals with a common purpose, the destruction of all organized society; Japanese Radicals are not at all uncommon.

But what was this the Jap girl was doing? She had overturned the pile of deer skins and was attempting to reach to the bottom of the Russian's sleeping bag. Failing in this, she gave it a number of punches. With a keen glance toward the entrance she at last darted head foremost into the bag, much as a mouse would have gone into a boot.

She came out almost at once. Her hands were empty. Evidently the thing she sought was not there. Next she attacked a bundle, which Johnny recognized as part of the Russian's equipment. She had examined this and was about to put it in shape again when there came the faint shuffle of feet at the entrance. With one wild look about her, she darted to the pile of deer skins and disappeared beneath it.

She was not a moment too soon, for instantly the sharp chin and the sullen brow of the Russian appeared at the entrance.

When he saw the bundle in disorder, he sprang to the center of the room. His hand on his belt, he stared about the place for a second, then much as a cat springs at a tuft of grass where a mole is concealed, he sprang at the pile of deer skins.

Johnny's lips parted, but he uttered not a sound. His hand gripped the blue automatic. If the Russian found her, there would be no more Russian, that was all.

But to his intense surprise, he saw that as the man tore angrily at the pile, he uncovered nothing but skins.

Johnny smothered a sigh of relief which was mixed with a gasp of admiration. The girl was clever, he was obliged to admit that. In a period only of seconds, she had cut away the rope which bound the skin wall to the floor and had crept under the wall to freedom.

As Johnny settled back to watch, his brain was puzzled by one question; what was it that the Jap girl sought? Was it certain papers which the Russian carried, or was it—was it something which Johnny himself carried in his pocket at this very moment—the diamonds?

This last thought caused him a twinge of discomfort. If she was searching for the diamonds, could it be that they rightfully belonged to her or to her family, and had they been taken by the Russian? Or had the girl merely learned that the Russian had the jewels and had she followed him all this way with the purpose of robbing him? If the first supposition was correct, ought Johnny not to go to her and tell her that he had the diamonds? If, on the other hand, she was seeking possession of that which did not rightfully belong to her, would she not take them from him anyway and leave him to face dire results? For, though no law existed which would hold him responsible for the jewels, obtained as they had been under such unusual conditions, still Johnny knew all too well that the world organization of Radicals to which this Russian belonged had a system of laws and modes of punishment all its own, and, if the Russian succeeded in making his way to America and if he, Johnny, did not give proper account of these diamonds, sooner or later, punishment would be meted out to him, and that not the least written in the code of the Radical world.

He dismissed the subject from his mind for the time and gave his whole attention to the Russian. But that gentleman, after evincing his exceeding displeasure by kicking his sleeping bag about the room for a time, at last removed his outer garments, crept into the bag and went to sleep.

One other visit Johnny made that night. As the result of it he did not sleep for three hours after he had let down the deer skin curtain to his sleeping compartment.

"Hanada! Hanada?" he kept repeating to himself. "Of all the Japs in all the world! To meet him here! And not to have known him. It's preposterous."

Johnny had gone to the igloo now occupied by Iyok-ok. He had gone, not to spy on his friend, but to talk to him about recent developments and to ascertain, if possible, when they would cross the Strait. He had got as far as the tent flaps, had peered within for a few moments and had come away again walking as a man in his dream.

What he had seen was apparently not so startling either. It was no more than the boy with his parka off. But that was quite enough. Iyok-ok was dressed in a suit of purple pajamas and was turned half about in such a manner that Johnny had seen his right shoulder. On it was a three-cornered, jagged scar.

This scar had told the story. The boy was not an Eskimo but a Jap masquerading as an Eskimo. Furthermore, and this is the part which gave Johnny the start, this Jap was none other than Hanada, his schoolmate of other days; a boy to whom he owed much, perhaps his very life.

"Hanada!" he repeated again, as he turned beneath the furs. How well he remembered that fight. Even then—it was his first year in a military preparatory school—he had shown his tendencies to develop as a featherweight champion. And this tendency had come near to ending his career. The military school was one of those in which the higher classmen treated the beginners rough. Johnny had resented this treatment and had been set upon by four husky lads in the darkness. He had settled two of them, knocked them cold. But the other two had got him down, and were beating the life out of him when this little Jap, Hanada, had appeared on the scene. Being also a first year student, he had come in with his ju'jut'su and between them they had won the battle, but not until the Jap had been hung over a picket fence with a jagged wound in his shoulder. It was the scar of that wound Johnny had seen and it was that scar which had told him that this must be Hanada.

He smiled now, as he thought how he had taken Hanada to his room after that boy's battle and had attempted to sew up the cut with an ordinary needle. He smiled grimly as he thought of the fight and how he had resolved to win or die. Hanada had helped him win.

And here he had been traveling with the Japanese days on end and had not recognized him. And yet it was not so strange. He had not seen him for six years. Had Hanada recognized him? If he had, and Johnny found it hard to doubt it, then he had his own reasons for keeping silent. Johnny decided that he would not be the first to break the silence. But after all there was a strange new comfort in the realization that here was one among all these strangers whom he could trust implicitly. And Hanada would make a capital companion with whom he might cross the thirty-five miles of drifting, piling ice which still lay between him and America. It was the contemplation of these realities which at last led him to the land of dreams.

CHAPTER IX

JOHNNY'S FREE-FOR-ALL

Johnny smiled as he sat before his igloo. Two signs of spring pleased him. Some tiny icicles had formed on the cliff above him, telling of the first thaw. An aged Chukche, toothless, and blind, had unwrapped his long-stemmed pipe to smoke in the sunshine.

Johnny had seen the old man before and liked him. He was cheerful and interesting to talk to.

"See that old man there?" he asked Hanada, whom he still called Iyok-ok when speaking to him. "Communism isn't so bad for him after all."

Hanada squinted at him curiously without speaking.

"Of course, you know," said Johnny, "what these people have here is the communal form of government, or the tribal form. Everything belongs to the tribe. They own it in common. If I kill a white bear, a walrus or a reindeer, it doesn't all go in my storehouse. I pass it round. It goes to the tribe. So does every other form of wealth they have. Nothing belongs to anyone. Everything belongs to everybody. So, when my old friend gets too old to hunt, fish or mend nets, he basks in the sun and needn't worry about anything at all. Pretty soft. Perhaps our friend the Russian is not so far wrong after all if he's a communist."

"Uh-hu," the Jap grunted; then he exclaimed, "That reminds me, Terogloona, the Chukche who lives three doors from here, asked me to tell you to stay out of his igloo this afternoon."

"Why?"

The Jap merely shrugged his shoulders.

"I have a way of doing what I am told not to, you should—" Johnny was about to say, "you should know that," but checked himself in time.

"Better not go," warned Hanada as he turned away.

After an early noon lunch Johnny strolled up the hill top. He wanted to get a view of the Strait. On particularly clear days, Cape Prince of Wales on the American side of Behring Strait can be seen from East Cape in Siberia. This day was clear, and, as Johnny climbed, he saw more and more of the peak as it lay across the Strait, above the white ice floes.

With trembling fingers he drew a one dollar bill from his pocket and spread it on his knee. "There it is," he whispered. "There's the place where you came from, little old one-spot. And I am going to take you back there. The Wandering Jew once stood here and saw his sweetheart in a mirage on the other side. He was afraid to cross. But he only had a sweetheart to call him. We've got that and a lot more. We've got a country calling us, the brightest, the best country on the map. And we dare try to go back. Once that dark line of water disappears we'll be going."

Then questions began to crowd his brain. Would Hanada attempt the Strait at this time? What was his game anyway? Was he a member of the Japanese secret service detailed to follow the Russian, or was he traveling of his own accord? Except by special arrangement Japanese might not come to America. Was Hanada sneaking back this way? It did not seem like him. Perhaps he would not cross at all.

Johnny's eyes once more swept the broad expanse of drifting ice. Then his gaze became riveted on one spot. The band of black water had narrowed to a ribbon. This meant an onshore wind. Soon they would be able to cross from the solid shore ice to the drifting floe. Surely there could be no better time to cross the Strait. With the air clear and wind light, the crossing might be made in safety.

Even as he looked, Johnny saw a man leap the gap. Curiosity caused him to watch this man, whom he had taken for a Chukche hunter. Now he appeared, now disappeared, only to reappear again round an ice pile. But he behaved strangely for a hunter. Turning neither to right nor left, except to dodge ice piles, he forged straight ahead, as if guided by a compass. Soon it became apparent that he was starting on the trip across the Strait. Chukches did not attempt this journey. They had not sufficient incentive. Could it be the Russian? Johnny decided he must hurry down and tell Hanada. But, even as he rose, he saw a second person leap across the gap in the ice. This one at once started to trail the first man. There could be no mistaking that youthful springing step. It was Hanada in pursuit.

With cold perspiration springing out on his forehead, Johnny sat weakly down. He was being left behind, left behind by his friend, his classmate, the man who above all men he had thought could be depended upon. How could he interpret this?

For a time Johnny sat in gloomy silence, trying to form an answer to the problem; trying also to map out a program of his own.

Suddenly he sprang to his feet. He had remembered that there was some sort of party down in the village, which he had been invited not to attend, and he had meant to go. Perhaps it was not too late if he hurried. He raced down the hill and straight to the igloo he had been warned against entering. A strapping young buck was standing guard at the flaps.

"No go," he said as Johnny approached.

"Go," answered Johnny.

"No go," said the native, his voice rising.

"Go," retorted Johnny quietly.

He moved to pass the native. The latter put his hand out, and the next instant felt himself whirled about and shot spinning down the short steep slope which led from the igloo entrance. Johnny's good right arm had done that.

As the American lad pushed back the flaps of the igloo and entered he stared for one brief second. Then he let out a howl and lunged forward. Before him, in the center of the igloo stood the old man who had been so peacefully smoking his pipe two hours before. He was now standing on a box which raised him some three feet from the floor. About his neck was a skin rope. The rope, a strong one, was fastened securely to the cross poles of the igloo. A younger man had been about to kick the box away.

This same younger man suddenly felt the jar of something hard. It struck his chin. After that he felt nothing.

The fight was on. There were a dozen natives in the room. A brawny buck with a livid scar on his right cheek lunged at Johnny. He speedily joined his friend in oblivion. A third man leaped upon Johnny's back. Johnny went over like a bucking pony. Finally landing feet first upon the other's abdomen, he left him to groan for breath. A little fellow sprang at him. Johnny opened his hand and slapped him nearly through the skin wall. They came; they went; until at last, very much surprised and quite satisfied, they allowed Johnny to cut the skin rope and help his old blind friend down.

A boy poked his head in at the flap. He had been a whaler and could speak English. He surveyed the room in silence for a moment, taking in each prostrate native.

"Now you have spoiled it," he told Johnny with a smile.

"I should say myself that I'd messed things up a bit," Johnny admitted, "but tell me what it's all about. What did the poor old cuss do?"

"Do?" the boy looked puzzled. "That one do?"

"Sure. What did they want to hang him for? He was too old and feeble to do anything very terrible; besides he's blind."

"Oh," said the boy smiling again. "He done not anything. Too old, that why. No work. All time eat. Better dead. That way think all my people. All time that way."

Johnny looked at him in astonishment, then he said slowly:

"I guess I get you. In this commune, this tribe of yours, everyone does the best he can for the gang. When he is too old to work, fish or hunt, the best thing he can do is die, so you hang him. Am I right?"

"Sure a thing," replied the boy. "That's just it."

Johnny shot back:

"No enjoying a ripe old age in this commune business?"

"No. Oh, no."

"Then I'm off this commune stuff forever," exclaimed Johnny. "The old order of things like we got back in the States is good enough for me. And, I guess it's not so old after all. It's about the newest thing there is. This commune business belongs back in the stone age when primitive tribes were all the organizations there were."

He had addressed this speech to no one in particular. He now turned to the boy, a black frown on his brow.

"See here," he said sharply, "this man, no die, See? Live. See? All time live, see? No kill. You tell those guys that. Tell them I mebby come back one winter, one summer. Come back. Old man dead. I kill three of them. See?"

Johnny took out his automatic and played with it longingly.

"Tell them if they don't act as if they mean to do what I say, I'll shoot them now, three of them."

The boy interpreted this speech. Some of the men turned pale beneath their brown skins; some shifted uneasily. They all answered quickly.

"They say, all right," the boy explained solemnly. "Say that one, if had known you so very much like old man, no want-a hang that one."

"All right." Johnny smiled as he bowed himself out.

It was the first near-hanging he had ever attended and he hoped it would be the last. But as he came out into the clear afternoon air he drank in three full breaths, then said, slowly:

"Communism! Bah!"

Hardly had he said this than he began to realize that he had a move coming and a speedy one. He was in the real, the original, the only genuine No Man's Land in the world. He was under the protection of no flag. The only law in force here was the law of the tribe. He had violated that law, defied it. He actually, for the moment, had set himself up as a dictator.

"Gee!" he muttered. "Wish I had time to be their king!"

But he didn't have time, for in the first place, all the pangs of past homesick days were returning to urge him across the Strait. In the second place the mystery of the Russian and Hanada's relation to him was calling for that action. And, in the third place, much as he might enjoy being king of the Chukches, he was quite sure he would never be offered that job. There would be reactions from this day's business. The council of headmen would be called. Johnny would be discussed. He had committed an act of diplomatic indiscretion. He might be asked to leave these shores; and then again an executioner might be appointed for him, and a walrus lance thrust through his back.

Yes, he would move. But first he must see the Jap girl and ask about her plans. It would not do to desert her. Hurrying down the snow path, he came upon her at the entrance to her igloo.

Together they entered, and, sitting cross-legged on the deer skins by the seal oil lamp, they discussed their futures.

The girl made a rather pitiful figure as she sat there in the glow of the yellow light. Much of her splendid "pep" seemed to have oozed away.

As Johnny questioned her, she answered quite frankly. No, she would not attempt to cross the Strait on the ice. It would be quite dangerous, and, beside, she had promised to stay. She did not say the promise had been made to Hanada but Johnny guessed that. Evidently they had thought the Russian might return. She told her American friend that she was afraid that her mission in the far north had met with failure. She would not tell what that mission was, but admitted this much: she had once been very rich, or her family had. Her father had been a merchant living in one of the inland cities of Russia. The war had come and then the revolution. The revolutionists had taken all that her father owned. He had died from worry and exposure, and she had been left alone. Her occupation at present was, well, just what he saw. She shrugged her shoulders and said no more.

Johnny with his natural generosity tried to press his roll of American money upon her. She refused to accept it, but gave him a rare smile. She had money enough for her immediate need and a diamond or two. Perhaps when the Strait opened up she would come by gasoline schooner to America.

Her mention of diamonds made Johnny jump. He instantly thought of the diamonds in his pocket. Could it be that her father had converted his wealth into diamonds and then had been robbed by the Radical revolutionist? He was on the point of showing the diamonds to her when discretion won the upper hand. He thought once more of the cruel revenges meted out by these Radicals. Should he give the diamonds to one to whom they did not belong, the penalty would be swift and sure.

Johnny did, however, press into her hand a card with his name and a certain address in Chicago written upon it and he did urge her to come there should she visit America.

He had hardly left the igloo when a startling question came to his mind. Why had the Russian gone away without further attempt to recover the treasure now in Johnny's possession? He had indeed twice searched the American's igloo in his absence and once had made an unsuccessful attack upon his person. He had gained nothing. The diamonds were still safe in Johnny's pocket. What could cause the man to abandon them? Here, indeed, must be one of the big men of the cult, perhaps the master of them all.

With this thought came another, which left Johnny cold. The cult had spies and avengers everywhere. They were numerous in the United States. They could afford to wait. Johnny could be trusted to cross the Strait soon. There would be time enough then. His every move would be watched, and when the time was ripe there would be a battle for the treasure.

That night, by the light of the glorious Arctic moon Johnny found his way across the solid shore ice and climbed upon the drifting floes, which were even now shifting and slowly piling. He was on his way to America. Perhaps he was the first American to walk from the old world to his native land. Certainly, he had never attempted thirty-five miles of travel which was fraught with so many perils.

CHAPTER X

THE JAP GIRL IN PERIL

Hardly had Johnny made his way across the shore ice and begun his dangerous journey when things of a startling nature began to happen to the Jap girl.

She was seated in her igloo sewing a garment of eider duck skins, when three rough-looking Chukches entered and, without ceremony, told her by signs that she must accompany them.

She was conducted to the largest igloo in the village. This she found crowded with natives, mostly men. She was led to the center of the floor, which was vacant, the natives being ranged round the sides of the place.

Instantly her eyes searched the frowning faces about her for a clue to this move. She soon found it. In the throng, she recognized five of the reindeer Chukches, members of that band which had attempted to murder Johnny Thompson and herself.

Their presence startled her. That they would make their way this far north, when their reindeer had been sent back by paid messengers some days before, had certainly seemed very improbable both to Johnny and to the girl.

Evidently the Chukches were very revengeful in spirit or very faithful in the performance of murders they had covenanted to commit. At any rate, here they were. And the girl did not deceive herself, this was a council chamber. She did not doubt for a moment that her sentence would be death. Her only question was, could there be a way of escape? The wall was lined with dusky forms this time. The entrance was closely guarded. Only one possibility offered; above her head, some five feet, a strong rawhide rope crossed from pole to pole of the igloo. Directly above this was the smoke hole. She had once entered one of these when an igloo was drifted over with snow.

The solemn parley of the council soon began. Like a lawyer presenting his case, the headman of the reindeer tribe stood before them all and with many gestures told his story. At intervals in his speech two men stepped forward for examination. The jaw of one of them was very stiff and three of his teeth were gone. As to the other, his face was still tied up in bandages of tanned deer skin. His jaw was said to be broken. The Jap girl, in spite of her peril, smiled. Johnny had done his work well.

There followed long harangues by other members of the reindeer tribe. The last speech was made by the headman of East Cape. It was the longest of all.

At length a native boy turned to the Jap girl and spoke to her in English.

"They say, that one; they say all; you die. What you say?"

"I say want—a—die," she replied smiling.

This answer, when interpreted, brought forth many a grunt of surprise.

"They say, that one! they say all," the boy went on, "how you want—a die? Shoot? Stab?"

"Shoot." She smiled again, then, "But first I do two thing. I sing. I dance. My people alletime so."

"Ki-ke" (go ahead) came in a chorus when her words had been interpreted.

No people are fonder of rhythmic motion and dreamy chanting than are the natives of the far north. The keen-witted Japanese girl had learned this by watching their native dancing. She had once visited an island in the Pacific and had learned while there a weird song and a wild, whirling dance.

Now, as she stood up she kicked from her feet the clumsy deer skin boots and, from beneath her parka extracted grass slippers light as silk. Then, standing on tip toe with arms outspread, like a bird about to fly, she bent her supple body forward, backward and to one side. Waving her arms up and down she chanted in a low, monotonous and dreamy tone.

All eyes were upon her. All ears were alert to every note of the chant. Great was the Chukche who learned some new chant, introduced some unfamiliar dance. Great would he be who remembered this song and dance when this woman was dead.

The tones of the singer became more distinct, her voice rose and fell. Her feet began to move, slowly at first, then rapidly and yet more rapidly. Now she became an animated voice of stirring chant, a whirling personification of rhythm.

And now, again, the song died away; the motion grew slower and slower, until at last she stood before them motionless and panting.

"Ke-ke! Ke-ke!" (More! More!) they shouted, in their excitement, forgetting that this was a dance of death.

Tearing the deer skin parka from her shoulders and standing before them in her purple pajamas, she began again the motion and the song. Slow, dreamy, fantastic was the dance and with it a chant as weird as the song of the north wind. "Woo-woo-woo." It grew in volume. The motion quickened. Her feet touched the floor as lightly as feathers. Her swaying arms made a circle of purple about her. Then, as she spun round and round, her whole body seemed a purple pillar of fire.

At that instant a strange thing happened. As the natives, their minds completely absorbed by the spell of the dance, watched and listened, they saw the purple pillar rise suddenly toward the ceiling. Nor did it pause, but mounting straight up, with a vaulting whirl disappeared from sight.

Overcome by the hypnotic spell of the dance, the natives sat motionless for a moment. Then the bark of a dog outside broke the spell. With a mad shout: "Pee-le-uk-tuk Pee-le-uk-tuk!" (Gone! Gone!) they rushed to the entrance, trampling upon and hindering one another in their haste.

*   *   *   *   *

When Johnny reached the piling ice, on his way across the Strait, he at first gave his entire attention to picking a pathway. Indeed this was quite necessary, for here a great pan of ice, thirty yards square and eight feet thick, glided upon another of the same tremendous proportions to rear into the air and crumble down, a ponderous avalanche of ice cakes and snow. He must leap nimbly from cake to cake. He must take advantage of every rise and fall of the heaving swells which disturbed the great blanket winter had cast upon the bosom of the deep.

All this Johnny knew well. Guided only by the direction taken by the moving cakes, he made his way across this danger zone, and out upon the great floe, which though still drifting slowly northward, did not pile and seemed as motionless as the shore ice itself.

While at the village at East Cape Johnny had made good use of his time. He had located accurately the position of the Diomede Islands, half way station in the Strait. He had studied the rate of the ice's drift northward. He now was in a position to know, approximately, how far he might go due east and how much he must veer to the south to counteract the drift of the ice. He soon reckoned that he would make three miles an hour over the uneven surface of the floe. He also reckoned that the floe was making one mile per hour due north. He must then, for every mile he traveled going east, do one mile to the south. He did this by going a full hour's travel east, then one-third of an hour south.

So sure was he of his directions that he did not look up until the rocky cliffs of Big Diomede Island loomed almost directly above him.

There was a native village on this island where he hoped to find food and rest and, perhaps, some news of the Russian and Hanada. He located the village at last on a southern slope. This village, as he knew, consisted of igloos of rock. Only poles protruding from the rocks told him of its location.

As he climbed the path to the slope he was surprised to be greeted only by women and children. They seemed particularly unkempt and dirty. At last, at the crest of the hill, he came upon a strange picture. A young native woman tastily dressed was standing before her house, puffing a turkish cigaret. She was a half-breed of the Spanish type, and Johnny could imagine that some Spanish buccaneer, pausing at this desolate island to hide his gold, had become her father.

She asked him into an igloo and made tea for him, talking all the while in broken English. She had learned the language, she told him, from the whalers. She spoke cheerfully and answered his questions frankly. Yes, his two friends had been here. They had gone, perhaps; she did not know. Yes, he might cross to Cape Prince of Wales in safety she thought. But Johnny had the feeling that her mind was filled with the dread of some impending catastrophe which perhaps he might help avert.

And at last the revelation came. Lighting a fresh cigaret, she leaned back among the deer skins and spoke. "The men of the village," she said, "you have not asked me about them."

"Thought they were hunting," replied Johnny.

"Hunting, no!" she exclaimed. "Boiling hooch."

Johnny knew in a moment what she meant. "Hooch" was whisky, moonshine. Many times he had heard of this vicious liquor which the Eskimos and Chukches concocted by boiling sourdough, made of molasses, flour and yeast.

The girl told him frankly of the many carouses that had taken place during the winter, of the deaths that had resulted from it, of the shooting of her only brother by a drink-crazed native.

Johnny listened in silence. That she told it all without apparent emotion did not deceive him. Hooch was being brewed now. She wished it destroyed. This was the last brew, for no more molasses and flour remained in the village. This last drunken madness would be the most terrible of all. She told him finally of the igloo where all the men had gathered.

Johnny pondered a while in silence. He was forever taking over the troubles of others. How could he help this girl, and save himself from harm? What could he do anyway? One could not steal four gallons of liquor before thirty or forty pairs of eyes.

Suddenly, an idea came to him. Begging a cigaret from the native beauty, he lighted it and gave it three puffs. No, Johnny did not smoke. He was merely experimenting. He wanted to see if it would make him sick. Three puffs didn't, so having begged another "pill" and two matches he left the room saying:

"I'll take a look."

*   *   *   *   *

When the Jap girl leaped through the smoke hole of the igloo at East Cape she rolled like a purple ball off the roof. Jumping to her feet she darted down the row of igloos. Pausing for a dash into an igloo, she emerged a moment later bearing under one arm a pile of fur garments and under the other some native hunting implements. Then she made a dash for the shore ice.

It was at this juncture that the first Chukche emerged from the large igloo. At his heels roared the whole gang. Like a pack of bloodthirsty hounds, they strove each one to keep first place in the race. Their grimy hands itched for a touch of that flying girlish figure.

Though she was a good quarter mile in the lead she was hampered by the articles she carried. Certain young Chukches, too, were noted for their speed. Could she make it? There was a full mile of level, sandy beach and quite as level shore ice to be crossed before she could reach the protection of the up-turned and tumbled ice farther out to sea.

On they came. Now their cries sounded more distinctly; they were gaining. Now she heard the hoarse gasps of the foremost runner; now imagining that she felt his hot breath on her cheek she redoubled her energy. A grass slipper flew into the air. She ran on barefooted over the stinging ice.

Now an ice pile loomed very near. With a final dash she gained its shelter. With a whirl she darted from it to the next, then to the right, straight ahead, again to the right, then to the left. But even then she did not pause. She must lose herself completely in this labyrinth of up-ended ice cakes.

Five minutes more of dodging found her far from the shouting mob, that by this time was as hopelessly lost as dogs in a bramble patch.

The Jap girl smiled and shook her fist at the shore. She was safe. Compared to this tangled wilderness of ice, the Catacombs of Rome were an open street.

Throwing a fur garment on a cake of ice, she sat down upon it, at the same time hastily drawing a parka over her perspiring shoulders. She then proceeded to examine her collection of clothing. The examination revealed one fawn skin parka, one under suit of eider duck skin, one pair of seal skin trousers, two pairs of seal skin boots, with deer skin socks to match, and one pair of deer skin mittens. Besides these there was an undressed deer skin, a harpoon and a seal lance.

Not such a bad selection, this, for a moment's choosing. The principal difficulty was that the whole outfit had formerly belonged to a boy of fourteen. The Jap girl shrugged her shoulders at this and donned the clothing without compunctions.

When that task was complete she surveyed herself in an up-ended cake of blue ice and laughed. In this rig, with her hair closely plaited to her head, her own mother would have taken her for a young Chukche boy out for a hunt.

Other problems now claimed her attention. She was alone in the world without food or shelter. She dared not return to the village. Where should she go?

Again she shrugged her shoulders. She was warmly clad, but she was tired and sleepy. Seeking out a cubby hole made by tumbled cakes of ice, she plastered up the cracks between the cakes with snow until only one opening remained. Then, dragging her deer skin after her, she crept inside. She half closed the opening with a cake of snow, spread the deer skin on the ice and curled up to sleep as peacefully as if she were in her own home.

One little thing she had not reckoned with; she was now on the drifting ice of the ocean, and was moving steadily northward at the rate of one mile an hour.

CHAPTER XI

A FACE IN THE NIGHT

When Johnny left the igloo of the native girl he made his way directly up the hill for a distance of a hundred yards. Then, turning, he took three steps to the right and found himself facing the entrance to a second stone igloo. That it was an old one and somewhat out of repair was testified to by the fact that light came streaming through many a crevice between the stones.

Keeping well away from the entrance, Johnny took his place near one of these crevices. What he saw as he peered within would have made John Barleycorn turn green with envy. A moonshine still was in full operation. Beneath a great sheet iron vat a slow fire of driftwood burned. Extending from the vat was the barrel of a discarded rifle. This rifle barrel passed through a keg of ice. Beneath the outer end of the rifle barrel was a large copper-hooped keg which was nearly full of some transparent liquid. The liquid was still slowly dripping from the end of the rifle barrel.

That the liquid was at least seventy-five per cent alcohol Johnny knew right well. That it would soon cease to drip, he also knew; the fire was burning low and no more driftwood was to be seen.

Johnny sized up the situation carefully. Aside from some crude benches running round its walls and a cruder table which held the moonshine still, the room was devoid of furnishings. Ranged round the wall, with the benches for seats, were some thirty men and perhaps half as many hard-faced native women. On every face was an expression of gloating expectancy.

Now and again, a hand holding a small wooden cup would steal out toward the keg to be instantly knocked aside by a husky young fellow whose duty it appeared to be to guard the hooch.

Johnny tried to imagine what the result would be were he suddenly to enter the place. He would not risk that. He would wait. He counted the moments as the sound of the dripping liquid grew fainter and fainter. At last there came a loud:

"Dez-ra" (enough), from an old man in the corner.

Instantly the tank was lifted to one side, the fire beaten out, the keg of ice flung outside and the keg of hooch set on the table in the center of the room.

Everybody now bent eagerly forward as if for a spring. Every hand held a cup. But at this instant there came the shuffle of footsteps outside. Instantly every cup disappeared. The kettle was lifted to a dark corner. The room was silent when Johnny stepped inside.

"Hello," he shouted.

"Hello! Hello!" came from every corner.

"Where you come from?" asked the former tender of the still.

"East Cape."

"Where you go?"

"Cape Prince of Wales."

"Puck-mum-ie?" (Now?) The man betrayed his anxiety.

"Canak-ti-ma-na" (I don't know), said Johnny seating himself on the table and allowing his glance to sweep the place from corner to corner. "I don't know," he repeated, slowly. "How are you all anyway?"

"Ti-ma-na" (Not so bad), answered the spokesman.

Johnny was enjoying himself. He was exactly in the position of some good motherly soul who held a pumpkin pie before the eyes of several hungry boys. The only difference was that the pie Johnny was thinking of was raw, so exceeding raw that it would turn these natives into wild men. So Johnny decided that, like as not, he wouldn't let them have it at all.

Johnny enjoyed the situation nevertheless. He was mighty unpopular at that moment, he knew, but his unpopularity now was nothing to what it would be in a very short time. Thinking of this, he measured the distance to the door very carefully with his eye.

At last, when it became evident that if he didn't move someone else would, he turned to the still manager and said:

"Well, guess I'll be going. Got a match?"

He produced the borrowed cigaret. A sigh of hope escaped from the group of natives and a match was thrust upon him.

"Thanks."

The match was of the sulphur kind, the sort that never blow out.

Nonchalantly Johnny lighted the cigaret, then, all too carelessly, he flipped the match. Though it seemed a careless act, it was deftly done.

There came a sudden cry of alarm. But too late; the match dropped squarely into the keg of alcohol. The next instant the place was all alight with the blaze of the liquor, which flamed up like oil.

"This way out," exclaimed Johnny leading the procession for the door. Lightly he bounded down the hill. He caught one glimpse of the young woman as he passed, but this was no time for lingering farewells. The owner of the still was on his trail.

Dodging this way and that, sliding over a wide expanse of ice, Johnny at last eluded his pursuers in the wildly tumbled ice piles of the sea. As he paused to catch his breath he heard the soft pat-pat of a footstep and glancing up, caught a face peering at him round an ice pile.

"The Russian," he exclaimed.

*   *   *   *   *

When the Jap girl awoke after several hours of delicious sleep in her ice palace bedroom, she looked upon a world unknown. The sun was shining brightly. The air was clear. In a general way she knew the outline of East Cape and the Diomede Islands. She knew, too, where they should be located. It took her some time to discover them and when she did it was with a gasp of astonishment. They were behind her.

Realizing at once what had happened, she stood up and held her face to the air. The wind was off shore. There was not the least bit of use in trying to make the land. A stretch of black waters yawned between shore and ice floe by now.

Shrugging her shoulders, she climbed a pile of ice for a better view, then hurrying down again, she picked up the harpoon and began puzzling over it. She coiled and uncoiled the skin rope attached to it. She worked the rope up and down through the many buttons which held it to the shaft. She examined the sharp steel point of the shaft which was fastened to the skin rope.

After that she sat down to think. Over to the left of her she had seen something that lay near a pool of water. She had never hunted anything, did not fancy she'd like it, but she was hungry.

There was a level pan of ice by the pool. The creature lay on the ice pan. Suddenly she sprang up and made her way across the ice piles to the edge of that broad pan. The brown creature, a seal, still some distance away, did not move.

Searching the ice piles she at last found a regularly formed cake some eight inches thick and two feet square. With some difficulty she pried this out and stood it on edge. The edge was uneven, the cake tippy. Rolling it on its side she chipped it smooth with the point of the harpoon.

The second trial found the cake standing erect and solid. Gripping her harpoon, she threw herself flat on her stomach and pushing the cake before her, began to wriggle her way toward the sleeping seal.

Once she paused long enough to bore a peep hole through the cake with her dagger. From time to time the seal wakened, and raised his head to look about. Then he sank down again. Now she was but three rods away, now two, now one. Now she was within ten feet of the still motionless quarry.

Stretching every muscle for a spring like a cat, she suddenly darted forward. At the next instant she hurled the harpoon deep into the seal's side. She had him!

Through her body pulsated thrills of wild triumph which harkened back to the days of her primitive ancestry. Then for a second she wavered. She was a woman. But she was hungry. Tomorrow she might be starving.

Her knife flashed. A stream of red began dyeing the ice. A moment later, the creature's muscles relaxed.

The Japanese girl, Cio-Cio-San, sat up and began to think. Here was food, but how was it to be prepared? To think of eating raw seal meat was revolting, yet here on the floe there was neither stove nor fuel.

Slowly and carefully she stripped the skin from the carcass. Beneath this she found a two-inch layer of blubber, which must be more than ninety per cent oil. Under this was a compact mass of dark meat. This would be good if it was cooked. She sat down to think again. The fat seemed to offer a solution. It would burn if she had matches. She felt over the parka for pockets, and, with a little cry of joy, she found in one several matches wrapped in a bit of oiled seal skin. Every native carried them.

Hastily she stripped off a bit of fat and having lighted it, watched it flare up and burn rapidly. She laughed and clapped her hands.

But before she could cut off a bit of meat to roast over its flames, the soft ice began melting beneath it and the flames flickered out with a snapping flutter.

This would not do. There must be some other way found. Rising, she drove her harpoon into the snow at the crest of an ice pile. To this she fastened her deer skin, that it might act as a beacon to guide her back to her food supply. Then she turned about the ice pile and began wandering in search of she hardly knew what.

She at last came upon some old ice, with cakes ground round and discolored with age and then with a little cry of joy she started forward. The thing she saw had been discarded as worthless long ago; some gasoline schooner's crew had thrown it overboard. It was an empty five-gallon can which had once held gasoline. It was red with rust, but she pounced upon it and hurried away.

Once safely back at her lodge she used the harpoon to cut out a door in the upper end of the can. After cutting several holes in one side, she placed it on the ice with the perforated side up and put a strip of blubber within. This she lighted. It gave forth a smoky fire, with little heat, but much oil collected in the can. Seeing this, she began fraying out the silk ribbon of her pajamas. When she had secured a sufficient amount of fine fuzz she dropped it along the edge of the oil which saturated it at once. She lighted this, which had formed itself into a sort of wick, and at once she had a clear and steady flame.

She had solved the problem. In her seal oil oven, meat toasted beautifully. In half an hour she was enjoying a bountiful repast. After the feast, she sat down to think. She was fed for the moment and apparently safe enough, but where was she and whither was she being carried by this drifting ice floe?

*   *   *   *   *

For a second, after seeing the face of the Russian on the ice, Johnny Thompson stood motionless. Then he turned and ran, ran madly out among the ice piles. Heedless of direction he ran until he was out of breath and exhausted, until he had lost himself and the Russian completely.

No, Johnny was not running from the Russian. He was running from himself. When he saw the Russian's face, lit up as it was by the flare of the flames that had burst forth from that abandoned igloo, there had been something so crafty, so cruel, so remorselessly terrible about it that he had been seized with a mad desire to kill the man where he stood.

But Johnny felt, rather than knew, that there were very special reasons why the Russian must not be killed, at least not at that particular moment. Perhaps some dark secret was locked in his crafty brain, a secret which the world should know and which would die if he died. Johnny could only guess this, but whatever might be the reason he must not at this moment kill the man whom he suspected of twice attempting his life. So he fled.

By the last flickering flames of the grand spree that had burned, Johnny figured out his approximate location and began once more his three miles east, one mile south journey to Cape Prince of Wales. Some hours later, having landed safely at the Cape, and having displayed the postmarked one dollar bill to the post mistress and given it to her in exchange for a sumptuous meal of reindeer meat, hot biscuits and doughnuts, he started sleeping the clock round in a room that had been arranged for the benefit of weary travelers.

CHAPTER XII

"GET THAT MAN"

The trip from Cape Prince of Wales to Nome was fraught with many dangers. Already the spring thaw had begun. Had not the Eskimo whom Johnny employed to take him to the Arctic metropolis with his dog team been a marvel at skirting rotten ice and water holes in Port Clarence Bay, at swimming the floods on Tissure River, and at canoeing across the flooded Sinrock, Johnny might never have reached his journey's end.

As it was, two weeks from the time he left East Cape in Siberia, he stood on the sand spit at Nome, Alaska. By his side stood Hanada, who was still acting the part of an Eskimo and who had come down a few days ahead of him.

They were viewing a rare sight, the passing out to sea of the two miles of shore ice. The spring thaw had been followed by an off-shore wind which was carrying the loosened ice away. Johnny's interest was evenly divided between this rare spectacle and the recollection of the events that had recently transpired.

"Look!" said Hanada. "I believe the ice will carry the farther end of the cable tramway out to sea."

Johnny looked. It did seem that what the boy said was true. Already the cable appeared to be as tight as a fiddle string.

The tramway was a cable which stretched from a wooden tower set upon a stone pillar jutting from the sea to a similar tower built upon the land. This tramway, during the busy summer months of open sea, is used in lieu of a harbor and docks to bring freight and passengers ashore. This is done by drawing a swinging platform over the cable from tower to tower and back again. The platform at the present moment swung idly at the shore end of the cable. The beach had been fast locked in ice for eight months and more.

"Looks like it might go," said Johnny absentmindedly.

Neither he nor the Jap had seen or heard anything of the Russian. Two things would seem to indicate that that mysterious fugitive was in town; three times Johnny had found himself being closely watched by certain rough-looking Russian laborers, and once he had narrowly averted being attacked in a dark street at night by a gang of the same general character.

Hanada had not yet chosen to reveal his identity, and Johnny had not questioned him.

Only the day before a placard in the post office had given him a start. It was an advertisement offering a thousand dollars reward for knowledge which would lead to the arrest of a certain Russian Radical of much importance. This man was reported to have made his way through the Allied front near Vladivostok, and to have started north, apparently with the intention of crossing to America. To capture him, the placard declared, would be an act of practical patriotism.

Johnny had stared in wonder at the photograph attached. It was the likeness of a man much younger than the Russian they had followed so far, but there could be no mistaking that sharp chin and frowning brow. They had doubtless followed that very man for hundreds of miles only to lose him at this critical moment.

What had surprised him most of all had been the Jap's remark, as he read the notice:

"The blunderer! Wooden-headed blunderer!" Hanada had muttered as he read the printed words.

"Would you take him if you saw him?" Johnny had asked.

The Jap had turned a strangely inquiring glance at him, then answered:

"No!"

But they had not found him. And now the ice was going out. Soon ships would be coming and going. Little gasoline schooners would dash away to catch the cream of the coast-wise trading; great steamers would bring in coal, food, and men. In all this busy traffic, how easy it would be for the Russian to depart unseen.

Johnny sighed. He had grown exceedingly fond of dogging the track of that man. And besides, that thousand dollars would come in handy. He would dearly love to see the man behind prison bars. There would be no holding him for crimes he had attempted in Siberia, but probably the United States Government had something on him.

"Look!" exclaimed the Jap. "The tower has tipped a full five feet!" It was true. The ice crowding from the shore had blocked behind the tower, which stood several hundred feet from land. A dark line of water had opened between the two towers. Evidently the harbor committee would have some work on its hands.

"They're running down there," said Johnny, pointing to three men racing as if for their lives toward the shore tower. "Wonder what they think they can do?"

"Looks like the two behind were chasing the fellow in the lead," said Hanada.

"They are!" exclaimed Johnny. "Poor place for safety, I'd say, but he's got quite a lead."

At that instant the man in front disappeared behind the shore tower. As they watched, they saw a strange thing: the swinging platform began to move slowly along the rusty cable, and, just as it got under way, a man leaped out upon it.

"He's started the electric motor and is giving himself a ride," explained Johnny, "but if it's as bad as that, it must be pretty bad. He's desperate, that's all. The outer tower's likely to go over at any moment and dash him to death. Even if he makes it, where'll he be? Going out to sea on the floe, that's all."

Slowly the platform crept across the space over the black waters, then over the tumbling ice. The outer tower could be seen to dip in toward the shore. The cable sagged. The two other runners were nearing the inner tower.

"C'mon!" exclaimed Johnny, "The Golden West. A telescope!"

Closely followed by Hanada, he leaped away toward the hotel where, in a room especially prepared for it, was a huge brass telescope mounted on a tripod. Johnny, glancing out to sea, knew that the tower would be over in another thirty seconds. The platform was not twenty feet from its goal. His eye was now at the telescope. One second and he swung the instrument about. Then a gasp escaped his lips:

"The Russian!"

"The Russian?" Hanada snatched the telescope from him.

As Johnny watched he saw the man leap just as the platform lurched backward. The two men at the other tower had reversed the motor, but they were too late.

The next moment the outer tower toppled into the sea; the cable cut the water with a resounding swish. Johnny saw the Russian leap from ice cake to ice cake until at last he disappeared behind a giant pile, safe on a broad field of solid ice.

Hanada sat down. His face was white.

"Gone!" he muttered hoarsely.

"A boat?" suggested Johnny.

"No good. The ice floe's two miles wide, forty miles long and all piled up. Couldn't find him. He'd never give himself up. But he'll come back."

"How?"

"I don't know, but he'll come. You'll see. He's a devil, that one. But we'll get him yet."

"And the thousand," suggested Johnny.

Hanada looked at him in disgust. "A thousand dollars! What is that?"

"Is it as bad as that?" Johnny smiled in spite of himself.

"Yes, and worse, many times worse. I tell you, we must get that man! When the time comes, we must get him, or it will be worse for your country and mine."

"Ours is the same country," suggested Johnny.

"Huh!" Hanada shrugged his shoulders. "I am Hanada, your old schoolmate, now a member of the Japanese Secret Police, and you are Johnny Thompson. Whatever else you are, I don't know. The Russian has left us for a time. Let's talk about those old school days, and forget."

And they did.

CHAPTER XIII

BACK TO OLD CHICAGO

In the spring all the ice from upper Behring Sea passes through Behring Strait. One by one, like squadrons of great ships, floes from the shores of Cape York, Cape Nome and the Yukon flats drift majestically through that narrow channel to the broad Arctic Ocean.

So it happened that in due time the ice floe on which the Russian had sought refuge drifted past the Diomede Islands and farther out, well into the Arctic Ocean, met the floe on which the Jap girl had been lost as it circled to the east.

All ignorant of the passenger it carried, the girl welcomed this addition to her broad domain of ice. She had lived on the floe for days, killing seal for her food and melting snow to quench her thirst. But of late the cakes had begun to drift apart. There was danger that the great pan on which she had established herself would drift away from the others, and, in that case, if no seals came, she would starve. This new floe crowded upon hers and made the one on which she camped a solid mass again.

Spying some strange, dark spots on the newly arrived floe, she hurried over to the place and was surprised to find that it was a great heap of rubbish carted from some city. Though she did not know it, she guessed that city was Nome.

With the keen pleasure of a child she explored the heaps, selecting here a broken knife, there a discarded kettle, and again some other utensil which would help her in setting up a convenient kitchen.

But it was as she made her way back to her camp that she received the greatest shock. Suddenly, as she rounded a cake of ice, she came upon a man sprawled upon the ice, as if dead. The girl took no chances. In the land whence she came, it was not considered possible that this man should die. She sprang between two up-ended cakes, and from this shelter studied him cautiously. Yes, there was no mistaking him; it was the Russian. A slight movement of one arm told her he was not dead. Whether he was unconscious or was sleeping she could not tell.

Presently, after tying her dagger to her waist by a rawhide cord, she crept silently forward. An ear inclined toward his face told her that he was breathing regularly; he was sleeping the torpid sleep of one worn by exhaustion, exposure and starvation.

Ever so gently she touched him. He did not move. Then, with one hand on her dagger, she felt his clothing, as if searching for some object hidden in his fur garments. Her touch was light as a feather, yet she appeared to have a wonderful sense of location in the tips of those small, slender fingers.

Once the man moved and groaned. Light as a leaf she sprang away, the dagger gleaming in her hand. There were reasons why she did not wish to kill that man; other reasons than the fact that she was a woman and shrank from slaying, and yet she was in a perilous position. Should it come to a choice between killing him or suffering herself, she would kill him.

Again the man's body relaxed in slumber. Again she glided to his side and continued her search. When at last she straightened up, it was with a look of despair. The thing she sought was not there.

When the Russian awoke some time later it was with the feeling that he had been prodded in the side. The first sensation to greet him after that was the savory smell of cooked meat. Unable to believe his senses, he opened his eyes and sat up. Before him was a tin pan partly filled with strips of reddish-brown meat and squares of fried fat. The dish was still hot.

Like a dog that fears to have his food snatched from him, he glared about him and a sort of snarl escaped his lips. Then he fell upon the food and ate it ravenously. With the last morsel in his hand, he looked about him for signs of the human being who had befriended him. But in his eye was no sign of gratitude, rather the reverse—a burning fire of suspicion and hate lurked in their sullen depths. His gaze finally rested for a moment on the meat in his hand. Then his face blanched. The meat had been neatly cut by an instrument keen as a razor.

* * * * *

The steam-whaler, Karluke, a whole year overdue, pushing her way south through the ice-infested Strait, her crew half mutinous, and her food supply low, was subjected to two vexatious delays. Once she halted to pick up a man who signaled her from the top of a shattered tower of wood which topped an ice pile. The man was a Russian. Again, the boat paused to take on board a youth, whom they supposed to be a Chukche hunter who had been carried by the floes from his native shores.

The Russian paid them well for his passage to Seattle. The supposed Chukche was sent to the galley to become cook's helper.

This Chukche boy was no other than the Jap girl. She realized at once the position she was in; a perilous enough one, once her identity was disclosed, and she did all in her power to play the part of a Chukche boy. She drew maps on the deck to show the seamen that she was a member of the reindeer Chukche tribes, who spoke a different language from the hunting tribes, thus explaining why she could not converse freely with the veteran Arctic sailors who had learned Chukche on their many voyages. She was fortunate in immediately securing a cook's linen cap. This she wore tightly drawn down to her ears, covering her hair completely.

One thing she discovered the first night on board: The Russian had in his stateroom a bundle. This had been hidden when she searched him on the ice. To have a look into that bundle became her absorbing purpose. Three times she attempted to enter his stateroom. On the third attempt she did actually enter the room, but so narrowly escaped having her linen mask torn from her head and her identity revealed by the irate Russian, that she at last gave it up.

Upon docking at Seattle both the Russian and the girl mingled with the crowd on the dock and quickly disappeared.

The clerks in Roman & Lanford's department store were more than mildly curious regarding an Eskimo boy, who, entering their store that day and displaying a large roll of bills, demanded the best in women's wearing apparel. They had in stock a complete outfit, just the size that would fit the strange customer, who was no other than the Jap girl.

* * * * *

Johnny Thompson and Hanada, after two weeks of fruitless watching and waiting in Nome, took a steamer for Seattle. Johnny had not been in that city a day
when, while walking toward the Washington Hotel, he felt a light touch on his
arm, and turned to look into the beaming face of the Jap girl.

"You—you here?" he gasped in amazement.

"Yes."

"Why! You look grand," he assured her. "Regular American girl."

She blushed through her brown skin. Then her face took on a serious look:

"The Russian—" she began.

"Yes, the Russian!" exclaimed Johnny eagerly.

"He is here—no, not here. This morning he takes train for Chicago. To-night we
will follow. We will get that man, you and I, and—Iyok-ok." Her lips tripped over
the last word.

"Hanada," Johnny corrected.

"He has told you?"

"Yes, he is an old friend."

"And mine too. Good! To-night we will go. We will get that man. Three of us.
That bad one!"

"All right," said Johnny. "See you at the depot to-night."

"Wait," said the girl. Her hand still on his arm, she stood on her tiptoe and whispered in his ear:

"My name Cio-Cio-San; your friend, Hanada friend. Good-by." Then she was
gone.

Johnny walked to his hotel as in a dream. He had hoped to return to his den, his
job and to Mazie in Chicago, and in a quiet way, all mysteries dissolved, to live
his old happy life. But here were all the mysteries carrying him right to his own

city and promising to end—in what? Perhaps in some tremendous sensation. Who could tell? And the diamonds; what of them? He put his hand to his inner pocket; they were still there. Was he watched? Would he be followed? Even as he asked himself the question, he fancied that a dark form moved stealthily across the street.

"Well, anyway," he said to himself, "I can't desert my Jap friends. Besides, I don't want to."

*   *   *   *   *

"Chicago," said Hanada some time later, as Johnny related his conversation with Cio-Cio-San. "That means the end is near."

The end was not so near as he thought. When it came it was not, alas! to be for him the kind of end he fancied.

"All right," he said. "To-night we go to Chicago."

On the trip eastward from Seattle, Johnny slept much and talked little. The Jap girl and Hanada occupied compartments in different cars and appeared to wish to avoid being seen together or with Johnny. This, he concluded, was because there might be Russian Radicals on this very train. Johnny slept with the diamonds pressed against his chest and it was with a distinct sense of relief that he at last heard the hollow roar of the train as it passed over the street subways, for he knew this meant he was back in dear old Chicago, where he might have bitter enemies, but where also were many warm friends.

CHAPTER XIV

THE MYSTERY OF THE CHICAGO RIVER

Johnny Thompson dodged around a corner on West Ohio street, then walked hurriedly down Wells street. At a corner of the building which shadowed the river from the north he paused and listened; then with a quick wrench, he tore a door open, closed it hastily and silently, and was up the dusty stairs like a flash. At the top he waited and listened, then turning, made his way up two other flights, walked down a dark corridor, turned a key in a lock, threw the door open, closed it after him, scratched a match, lighted a gas lamp, then uttered a low "Whew!" at the dust that had accumulated everywhere.

Brushing off a chair, he sat down. For a few moments he sat there in silent reflection. Then rising, he extinguished the light, threw up the sash, unhooked some outer iron shutters, sent them jangling against the brick wall, and drawing his chair to the window, stared reflectively down into the sullen, murky waters of the river. At last he was back in Chicago!

The time had been when the fact that Johnny Thompson occupied this room was no secret to anyone who really wanted to know. Johnny had roomed here when he first came to Chicago as a boy, working for six dollars a week. When, in the years that followed, it had been discovered that Johnny was quick as a bobcat and packed a wallop; when Johnny began making easy money, and plenty of it, he had stuck to the old room that overlooked the river. When he had heard his country's call to go to war, he had paid three years' rent on the room and had locked the door. If he never came back, all good and well. If he did return, the old room would be waiting for him, the room and the river. Now here he was once more.

The river! The stream had always held a great fascination for him. Johnny had seen other rivers but to him none of them quite came up to the old Chicago. In its silent, sullen depths lay power and mystery. The Charles River of Boston Johnny had seen, and called it a place of play for college boys. The Seine of Paris was a thing of beauty, not of power. The Spokane was a noisy blusterer. But the old Chicago was a grim and silent toiler. It bore on its waters great scows, lake boats, snorting, smoking tugs, screaming fire boats and police boats. Then, too, it was a river of mysteries. Down into its murky depths no eye could peer to discover the hidden and mysterious burdens which it carried away toward the Father of Waters.

Yes, give Johnny the room by the old Chicago! It was dusty and grim; but tomorrow he would clean it thoroughly. Just now he wished merely to sit here and think for an hour.

The time had been when Johnny had not cared who saw him enter this haven; but to-day things were different. Since he had got into this affair with the Russian and his band he had had a feeling that he was being constantly watched.

There was little wonder at this, for did he not carry on his person forty thousand dollars' worth of rare gems? And did they not belong to someone else?

"To whom?" Johnny said the words aloud as he thought of it.

His mind turned to his Japanese comrades, the girl and the man. He had told neither of them about the diamonds. Perhaps he should have done so, and yet he felt a strange reticence in the matter.

He was to meet Hanada at eight o'clock. Hanada had never told him why they were pursuing the Russian; why he could not be killed in Siberia; why he must not be killed or arrested if seen now, until he, Hanada, said the word. He had not told why he thought that the Secret Service men had committed a blunder in offering a reward for the Russian's capture.

As Johnny thought of it he wondered if he were a fool for sticking to this affair into which he had been so blindly led. He had not shown himself to his old boss or to Mazie. To them he was dead. He had looked up the official record that very morning and had seen that he was reported "Missing in Vladivostok; probably dead."

Should he stick to the Russian's trail, a course which might lead to his death, or should he take the diamonds to a customs office and turn them in as smuggled goods, then tell Hanada he was off the hunt, was going back to his old job and Mazie? That would be a very easy thing to do; and to stick was fearfully hard. Yet the words of his long time friend, "Get that man, or it will be worse for your country and mine," still rang in his ears. Was it his patriotic duty to stick?

And if he decided to go on with it, should he go to Hanada and ask for a show-down, all cards on the table; or should he trust him to reveal the facts in the case little by little or all at once, as seemed wise to him? Well, he should see.

Then, for a half hour, Johnny gave himself over to the wild, boyish reveries which the city air and the lights flickering on the water awakened. At the end of that half hour he put on his hat and went out. He was to meet Hanada on the Wells street bridge. Where the Japanese was staying he did not know, but that it was with some fellow countrymen he did not doubt. Cio-Cio-San was staying with friends, students at the University. It had been arranged that the three of them should meet at odd times and various places to discuss matters relating to their danger-ous mission. In this way they hoped to throw members of the band of Radicals off their tracks.

Their conversation that night came to little. Hanada had found no trace of the Russian, nor had he come into contact with any other important Radicals since reaching Chicago. Johnny's report was quite as brief. Hanada showed no inclina-tion to reveal more regarding the matter, and Johnny did not question him. He had fully determined to see the thing through, cost what it might.

It was after a roundabout walk through the deserted streets of the business section of the city that they came to South Water street. This street, the noisiest and most crowded of all Chicago at certain hours, was now as silent and deserted as a vil-lage green at midnight. Here a late pedestrian hurried down its narrow walk: there some boatman loitered toward his craft in the river. But for these the street was deserted.

And it was here, of all places, that they experienced the first thrill of the night. A heavy step sounded on the pavement around the corner. The next instant a man appeared walking toward them. His face was obscured by shadows, but there was no mistaking that stride.

"That's our man," whispered Johnny.

"The Russian?" questioned Hanada in equally guarded tones.

There was not time for another word, for the man, having quickened his pace was abreast of them, past them and gone.

"I don't know. Couldn't see his face," whispered the Jap.

"Quick!" urged Johnny; "there's a short cut, an alley. We can meet him again under the arc light."

Down a dark alley they dashed. Crashing into a broken chicken crate, then sprinting through an open court, they came out on another alley, and then onto a street.

They had raced madly, but now as they came up short, panting, they saw no one. The man had disappeared.

Suddenly they heard steps on the cross street.

"Turned the corner," panted Johnny. "C'mon!"

Again they dashed ahead, slowing only as they reached the other street.

Sure enough, halfway down the block they saw their man. He was walking rapidly toward the bridge. Quickening their pace they followed.

Distinctly they saw the man go upon the bridge. Very plainly they heard every footstep on the echoing planks. Then, just as they were about to step upon the bridge, the footsteps ceased.

"Sh!" whispered Johnny, bringing his friend to a halt. "He's stopped; maybe laying for us."

For a minute they stood there. The lapping of the water was the only sound till, somewhere in the distance an elevated train rattled its way north.

"C'mon," said Johnny. "We've met that bird in worse places than this; we can meet him again."

But they did not meet him, although they walked the full length of the bridge. There was not a place on the whole structure where a man could hide, but they searched it thoroughly. Then Johnny searched the sides, the abutments. He sent the gleam of his powerful flashlight into the dark depths beneath, but all to no purpose. The man was gone.

"Humph!" said Johnny.

"Hisch!" breathed Hanada.

"Well, all I have to say," observed Johnny presently, "is that if the old Chicago River has that fellow, he'll be cast ashore. The good old Chicago doesn't associate with any such."

They stood there leaning on the wooden railing debating their next move, when a shot rang out. Instantly they dropped to the floor of the bridge. A bullet whizzed over their heads, then another and another. After that silence.

"Get you?" whispered Johnny.

"No. You?"

"Nope."

Then a long finger of light came feeling its way along the murky waters to rest on the bridge.

With a sigh of relief, Johnny saw that it came from a police-boat down stream. The light felt its way back and forth, back and forth across the river, then up to the bridge and across that. It came to rest as it glared into their eyes. It blinked one, two, three times, then went out.

"I'm glad they didn't hold it on us," breathed Johnny. "In that light anybody that wanted to could get a bead on us."

Hearing heavy, hurrying footsteps approaching, they stood up well back against the iron braces.

"Police!" whispered Johnny.

"You fellows shoot?" demanded one of the policemen as they came up and halted before the two boys.

"Nope," Johnny answered.

"No stallin' now."

"Search us," Johnny suggested. "The shots were fired at us, though where from, blessed if I know. Came right out of space. We'd just searched the bridge from end to end. Not a soul on it."

"What'd y' search it fer?"

"A man."

"W'at man?"

"That's it," Johnny evaded. "We wanted to know who he was."

The policemen conversed with one another in low tones for a moment.

"One of the bullets struck a cross-arm; I heard it," suggested Johnny. "You can look at that if it'll be any comfort to you."

The policeman grunted, then following Johnny's flashlight, examined the spot where the bullet had flaked the paint from the bridge iron.

"Hurum!" he grumbled. "That's queer. Bullet slid straight up the iron when it struck. Ordinarily that'd mean she was shot square against it from below and straight ahead, but that can't be, fer that brings her comin' direct out of the river, which ain't human, nor possible. There wasn't a boat nor a barge nor even a plank on the river when the searchlight flashed from the gray prowler; was there, Mike?"

"Not even a cork," said Mike.

"Well, anyway, that clears youse guys," grunted the leader. "Now you better beat it."

Bidding Hanada good night, Johnny walked across the bridge, around four blocks, then made a dash for his room. There was dust on his blankets, but he could shake it off. Anyway, he probably would not sleep much that night. Probably he would spend most of the night sitting by the window, listening to the lap of the waters of the old river and trying to solve the strange problem of the bullets fired apparently from the depths of the stream.

CHAPTER XV

THE CAT CRY OF THE UNDERWORLD

Dodging in front of a street car, Johnny turned abruptly to the right and trailed a taxi for half a block; then he shot across the sidewalk to the end of a dark alley. Then he flattened himself against the wall and listened. Yes, it came at last, the faint thud of cautious footsteps. He had not thrown the man off the scent.

"Well then, I will," he muttered, gritting his teeth. Johnny was a trifle out of sorts to-night. The chase annoyed him.

He dodged down the alley, then up a narrow court. Prying open the window of an empty building, he crept in and silently slid the sash back in its place. Tiptoeing across the hall with the lightness of a cat, he crept up the dusty stairs. One, two, three flights he ascended, then feeling for the rounds of a short ladder, he climbed still higher, to lift a trapdoor at last and creep out upon the roof.

Once there he skulked from chimney to chimney until he had crossed the flat roofs of three buildings. The third had a trapdoor close to a chimney. This he lifted, then dropped behind him. He was now in his own building. Panting a little from the exertion, he tiptoed down the hall, turned the key and entered his room.

Having made sure that the iron blinds were closed, he snapped on a light. His eyes, roving around the room, fell presently upon something white on the floor. Johnny could see his own name scrawled upon it. There were but a few people in all the world who knew that Johnny Thompson had ever lived here. Probably all of those who did know thought him dead and buried in Russia. Who had written this note? Friend or foe?

He tore open the envelope and glanced at the note. It came to the point with brutal frankness.

"Johnny Thompson: You are known to have in your possession rare gems which do not belong to you. You will please leave them on the doorstep of 316 North Bird place, and rap three times before you leave.

"If not—"

That was all, save that in place of a signature there was a splotch of red sealing wax. The wax had been stamped with an iron seal. The mark of the seal was that of the Radical Clan—the same as that on the envelope which contained the diamonds.

"And that, I suppose," whispered Johnny to himself, "means that if I do not leave the diamonds where I am told to I shall be flattened out like that drop of wax."

Switching out the light, he opened the blinds and took his old seat by the window. He was at once absorbed in thought. So all his dodging and twisting had not served to throw them off his track. They had discovered his den. And he must give up the diamonds and—

"If not—"

Those two words stood out as plainly before him as if they were flashed forth from an electric sign on the roof across the river.

He was half minded to give the diamonds up, but not to those rascals. No, he would allow one of their spies to trail him to the Custom House, and there, before the man's very eyes, Johnny would take out the envelope with the seal plainly showing, and hand the diamonds in as smuggled goods.

There was but one objection to this plan; he still had a strange fancy that someway Cio-Cio-San had a rightful interest in those gems. At least, he was not sure she did not have. Until he had determined the truth in this matter, he was loath to part with them.

But in keeping them he was taking a risk. He might be attacked and killed by that ruthless gang at any time.

For a long time he sat, staring down at the river. He was not in a happy mood. He was tired of all this trouble, fighting and mystery. On crowded State street that afternoon, he had seen Mazie. That made it worse. He had never seen her look so well. She had changed; grown older, and he thought a little sadder. Was the sadness caused by the fact that she believed him dead? He dared to hope so. All this filled him with a mad desire to touch her hand once more, to speak to her, to assure her in a score of ways that he was not dead.

Then Hanada had disappointed him. He had hoped they would meet again and have another conference that night; had hoped that the wise little Jap would have some solution of the mystery of the shots from the river, and the strange disappearance of the man they had taken to be the Russian. But Hanada had said "No." He had given no reason; had merely left things that way. Hanada had been like that always; he never explained. Perhaps he did have some other important engagement; then why could he not tell Johnny of it? Why all this constant enshrouding of affairs in mystery? What did he, Johnny, know about the whole business anyway? Not a thing. He was only assured by the Jap that it was his duty to stick on the trail of the Russian until it led somewhere in particular. He was not, in any circumstances, to have him arrested or killed without first consulting Hanada.

"What rot!"

Johnny got up and paced the floor. Then, suddenly realizing that there was no longer cause for secrecy as to his whereabouts, he threw on the light and swung a punching bag down from the wall.

This ancient bit of leather, which had hung unused for many months, gave forth a volley of dust at first. But soon it was sending resounding thwacks echoing down the hall from Johnny's right and left punch.

Johnny even smiled as he sat down after a fifteen minutes round with this old friend. He was greatly pleased at one thing; his left arm was now quite as good as his right.

As he sat there, still smiling, his eyes fell on that note which had been thrust under his door. A strange, wild impulse seized him.

"So they know where I stay," he muttered. "I'll see how near I can come to finding out where they are hiding."

Taking the envelope containing the diamonds from his pocket, he crowded it down into the depths of his clothing; then, snapping off the light, he went out.

Hastening down the street and across the bridge, he was soon threading deserted streets and dark alleys. In time he came out upon Bird place, a half street, ending in a wall. The passage was narrow, hardly more than an alley.

The night was exceptionally dark and the place cheerless—just the setting for a crime. Lights behind drawn shutters were few. Only the very wretched or very wicked haunted such habitations.

Hugging the wall, Johnny sidled along toward 316. He knew the spot exactly, for though Johnny had never been of the underworld, he had spent many a restless night prowling about in all parts of the city. Suddenly he flattened out in a doorway and stood motionless, breathing quietly.

Had he heard the faint pat-pat of footsteps? Had he caught the dark blue of a shadow on yonder wall? For a full three minutes he stood there; then hearing, seeing nothing more, he glided out and resumed his snake-like journey toward the door of 316.

This time he did not go far, for suddenly looming from dark doorways four huge forms sprang at him. Johnny understood it all in a moment. The note was but a trick. They had not intended to trust him to leave the diamonds. They did not live at 316 at all. They merely had meant to draw him to this dark alley, then to "get" him. Well, they would find him a tough nut to crack!

His right shot out, and a heavy bulk crashed to the pavement. His left swung and missed. A wild creature sprang at his throat. Johnny's mind worked like lightning. Four were too many. They would get him. He must have help. The cat cry of the underworld! He had known that cry two years before. He had many friends who would answer it. They had introduced themselves at his boxing bouts. They had liked him because he played a fair game and "packed a winning wallop." If any of them were near they would come to his aid.

Drawing a long breath, he let forth a piercing scream that rose and fell like the wail of a fire siren. At the same time he jabbed fiercely with his right. The man collapsed, but at that instant a third man struck Johnny on the head and, all but unconscious, he reeled and fell to the ground.

Faintly as in a dream, he heard guttural murmurs. He felt the buttons give as his coat was torn open. Then there came the ringing report of a shot from the distance.

"Da bolice!" came in a guttural mutter.

*   *   *   *   *

The reason Hanada would not meet Johnny on this particular night was that he had a pressing engagement with other persons. Just at seven o'clock he might have been seen emerging from an obscure street. He hailed a taxi-cab and getting in, drove due north across the river and straight on until, with a sharp turn to the right, he drove two blocks toward the lake, only to turn again to the right and cross the river again. He had gone south several blocks when suddenly signaling the driver to stop, he handed him a five-dollar bill and darted into the welcoming portals of a vast hotel.

The next moment he was crossing marble floors to enter a heavily carpeted parlor. This, too, he crossed. Then the walls of the room seemed to swallow him up.

In a small, dimly lighted anteroom his coat and hat were taken by a servant. He then stepped into a room where a round table was spread with spotless linen and rare silver. There were five chairs ranged around the table. Hanada frowned as he counted them.

"It seems," he murmured, "that the man who attends to the serving does not know that Hanada dines with the Big Five to-night. Ah well! There is time enough and room enough. We shall dine together; never fear."

He stepped back in the shadow of the heavy curtains and waited expectantly.

"The Big Five," he murmured. "Some of America's richest, surely Chicago's greatest millionaires. And Hanada dines with them. They will listen to him, too. They will hang on his word. The Big Five will listen. And if they say 'Yes,' if they do—" He drew in his breath sharply. "If they do we will set the world afire with a great, new thing. They have the money, which is power, and I have the knowledge, which is greater power."

There was a sound outside the door. A servant entered and, bowing deferentially, moved toward the table. He deftly rearranged the chairs and the silver. When he left, there were six places set. Hanada smiled.

Had one been permitted to look in upon the diners in this simply appointed room of one of America's great hotels that night, he might have wondered at the manner in which five of Chicago's great men hung upon the words of one little Japanese, who, now and then as he spoke, as if to indicate the vastness and grandeur of his theme, spread his hands forth in a broad gesture.

The meal ended, his speech concluded, all questions answered, he at last rose, and with a low bow said:

"And now, gentlemen, I leave the proposition with you. Please do not forget that it is a great and glorious venture; a new and glorious empire! An honor to your country and mine."

He was gone.

For some time the five men sat in silence. Then one of them spoke:

"Is he mad?"

"Are we all mad?" questioned a second. His voice was husky.

"Well," said a third, "it sounds like a dream, a dream of great possibilities. We must sleep over it."

Without another word they moved out of the room. The meeting, one of the most momentous in the history of the century, perhaps, was ended.

* * * * *

When Johnny Thompson heard the shot and the guttural mutter, "Da bolice!" he made a final effort to rally his senses and to put up a fight.

He did succeed in struggling to his knees, but to fight was unnecessary. Just as another shot sent echoes down the alley and a bullet sang over their heads, his assailants took to their heels.

A slight, slouching figure came gliding toward Johnny.

"Jerry the Rat!" he murmured; then to the man himself:

"So, it's you, Jerry. Haven't seen you for two years."

Through blear-eyes the little fellow surveyed Johnny for a second.

"Johnny Thompson, de clean guy wot packs a wallop!" he exclaimed. "Dere dey go! We can get 'em!" He pointed down the alley.

"Got a gun?" asked Johnny, standing a bit unsteadily.

"Two of 'em. C'mon. We ken git de yeggs yit."

Johnny grasped the gun held out to him and the next instant was following the strangely swift rat of the waterfront.

"Dere dey go!" exclaimed the little fellow.

Down an alley they rushed, then out on a broad, but dimly lighted street. They were gaining on the gang. They would overhaul them. There would be a battle. Johnny figured this out as he ran, and tried to discover the mechanism of his weapon.

But at that juncture the pursued ones dashed through an open window of a deserted building which flanked the river.

"Dere dey go! De cheap sluggers!" exclaimed Jerry.

Leaping across the street, he reached the window only a moment after the last of the four had slammed it down.

But the men had paused long enough to throw the catch. It took Jerry a full minute to break its grip.

When, at last, they vaulted cautiously over the sill and flashed their light about the interior, they found the place empty.

"Dey's flew de coop!" whispered Jerry. "Now wot's de chanst of dem makin' a clean git away?"

They made a hurried examination of all possible exits. All the window ledges and doorsills were so encrusted with dust that one passing through them would be sure to leave his mark. That is, all but one were. One windowsill had apparently been swept clean. But that window faced the river. As they threw it up, and looked down from its ledge, they saw only the murky waters of the river swirling beneath them.

Johnny studied the situation carefully, and the more he studied, the more baffled he became. If a boat had been tied to the windowsill there would have been marks on the casing. There were no such marks; yet, the fugitives had gone that way. He thought of the shots fired from the river the previous night and tried to connect the two. He could not make it out.

"Dey's gone!" said Jerry the Rat. "Did dey fleece y'?"

Johnny smiled. "They were trying to croak me, Jerry, and they nearly did it. Got a bump on my head big as a turkey buzzard's egg."

"Who wuz dey?"

"That's what I don't know altogether. Say, Jerry, are there some tough characters hanging around the river these days that ain't regular crooks?"

"Is dey? Dere's a mess of 'em!"

"Where do they stay?" asked Johnny eagerly.

"Dat's it." The little fellow scratched his head. "I bin skulkin' 'round 'em to find out. Sometimes I follers 'em, like now. Dey always drop out like this. Dey's queer. Dey ain't regular crooks, nor regular guys either. Dey's cookin' soup for sump'n big."

"That's what I think," said Johnny. "What are they like?

"Dey's five Roosians, three Heinies, one Wop, an' one Jap, I seen."

"Say, Jerry," said Johnny suddenly, "do you want to earn some honest money?"

"Not work?"

"No, spyin'."

"Not on me pals? Not on regular crooks?"

"No, on these queer ones."

"I'm on. Wot's de lay?"

"Find where they stay. Hunt them day and night till you do. Here's a twenty. There's more where that came from. There's a century note if you get them. Get me?"

The Rat ducked his head in assent.

"Then good night."

"Night," he mumbled.

They were out of the building now and Johnny made his way cautiously back to his room. He had had quite enough for one night. Once he paused to thrust his hand beneath his vest. Yes, the diamonds were still there. His assailants had not had time to find them. He was not sure whether he was glad or sorry.

CHAPTER XVI

CIO-CIO-SAN BETRAYED

Very alert, Johnny Thompson at the stroke of eight the next night crept from a narrow runway between two buildings and walked briskly down the street. He had reached the runway by a route known only to himself. He was sure that for a time, at least, he would not be followed. At last he reached the bridge which was coming to harbor many mysteries for him. Halfway across the span he paused, and sinking into the shadow of an iron girder, began watching the surface of the water.

He was, in fact, attempting to understand those murky depths. From his room he had detected a strange light. Either reflected on the water or shining up through it, this light appeared a pale yellow glow, such as he had often seen given off by the jelly fish in the Pacific. That there was no such jelly fish to be found in fresh water he knew quite well. And he had never in his life noticed that glow in the river.

Now, as he surveyed the surroundings, he realized that the light could not have been reflected from any illumination in street or building. The glow from the water had appeared close to the wall of the empty building through which his four assailants of the night before had made good their escape.

As he stood there, slouching in the shadows, Johnny gave a great start; the light had appeared again. Beyond question it was beneath the water, not shining upon it. From this vantage point the light seemed stronger. It appeared for a few seconds, then disappeared again. Johnny scratched his head. What could it mean? For some time he stood in a brown study, then he laughed silently to himself.

"Probably phosphorescent substances being sent out from the drainpipe of a factory or chemical laboratory," he decided.

At that instant he was all alert. His hand closed on his automatic. A stealthy footfall had sounded on the bridge.

"Oh! It's you," he whispered a moment later.

Hanada grinned as he gripped Johnny's hand. "Thought I might miss you," he whispered.

The two were soon engaged in animated conversation. Their talk had to do with Johnny's adventure of the night before and the information regarding the Radicals furnished by Jerry the Rat. Hanada appeared unduly excited at the news.

"It seems," said Johnny, "that there must be a national conference of Radicals meeting somewhere near this river. Perhaps our old friend, the Russian of Vladivostok, is a delegate."

Hanada shot him a swift glance, as if to say: "How much do you know about this matter anyway?"

But for some time the Japanese did not speak; then it was concerning an entirely different affair. Cio-Cio-San had been visited by a fellow countryman who, although wholly unknown to her, had appeared to know a great deal about her private business. He had informed her that she had, within the last year, been robbed of some very valuable property and professed to have a knowledge of its whereabouts. If she would accompany him he would see that it was restored to her. The actions of the man had aroused her suspicions and she had refused to go. However, she had asked him to give her a day to think it over. He was to return at nine this night.

"Some nifty little mind reader, that Jap," smiled Johnny. "Tell him to come round and locate my long lost uncle's buried treasure."

However, though he passed the matter off as a jest, he was doing some very serious thinking about this rather strange affair. He had never told Hanada about the diamonds. Neither had he told of the note which had been thrust under the door.

Now he remembered that Jerry the Rat had spoken of a Jap as a member of the Radicals, and he wondered if Cio-Cio-San's visitor was the same man. If that were so, then what was his game? Was he planning to lead Cio-Cio-San into a trap? Certainly if the treasure the strange Jap had spoken of as having been stolen from the Japanese girl was the envelope of diamonds, and they had hoped to recover them from Johnny that night, they would have no intention of restoring them to Cio-Cio-San.

"I'd advise her, if I were you," said Johnny slowly, "to find out as much as she can, and not take too many chances. The man may be one of the Radicals, and he may be using the supposed treasure as a decoy. At the same time, if she handles the affair discreetly enough, she may be able to assist you in locating the Russian and his band, which, I take it, is your chief end and aim in life just now."

Hanada sent him another penetrating glance. "You have guessed that much," he admitted. "Well, soon I may be able to tell you all. In the meantime, if you need more money to pay this Jerry—Jerry, what was it you called him?"

"Jerry the Rat."

"Yes, yes, Jerry the Rat. If you need more money for him, I can get you more, plenty more. But," the lines of his face grew tense, "we must find them and soon, or it may be too late. We must act quickly."

Hanada had not said one word of his affairs of the night before, nor did he now as they were about to part.

Dull and heavy, there came the tread of feet on the bridge.

"The police!" whispered Johnny.

Hanada seemed distinctly nervous.

As the two patrolmen came abreast of them one of them flashed his light.

Hanada cringed into the shadows.

"Well," said a deep voice, "here's luck! Youse guys come with us. Youse guys is wanted at the station."

"What for?" Johnny demanded.

"Youse guys know well enough. Treason, they call it."

"Treason?" Johnny gave a happy laugh. "Treason? They'll have hard work to prove that."

*   *   *   *   *

Had one been privileged to see Cio-Cio-San at the moment Johnny Thompson and his friend were arrested, he might easily have imagined that she was back in Japan. The room in which she paced anxiously back and forth was Japanese to the final detail. The floor was covered thickly with mattings and the walls, done in a pale blue, were hung everywhere with long scrolls of ancient Japanese origin. Here a silver stork stood in a pool of limpid blue; there a cherry orchard blossomed out with all the extravagant beauty of spring, and in the corner a pagoda, with sloping, red-tile roof and wide doors, proclaimed the fact that the Japanese were a people of art, even down to house building. Silk tapestries of varying tints hung about the room, while in the shadows a small heathen god smiled a perpetual smile.

But it was none of these things that the girl saw at that moment. This room, fitted up as it had been by rich Japanese students, most certainly had brought back fond memories of her own country. But at this instant, her eyes turned often to a screen behind which was a stand, and on that stand was a desk telephone.

Hanada had promised to consult Johnny Thompson regarding the strange proposition of the unknown Japanese. He had promised to call her at once; by eight-thirty at the latest. The stranger was to return for his answer at nine. It now lacked but ten minutes of that hour, and no call had come from Hanada. She could not, of course, know that the men on whom she depended for counsel were prisoners of the police. So she paced the floor and waited.

Five minutes to nine and yet no call. Wrinkles came to her forehead, her step grew more impatient.

"If he does not call, what shall I do?" she asked herself.

Then there came the sharp ring of the telephone. She sprang to the instrument, but the call was for another member of the club.

Three minutes in which to decide. She walked thoughtfully across the floor. Should she go? Her money was now almost gone. It was true that a treasure, which to many would seem a vast fortune, had disappeared from her father's house over night. It had been taken by force. And she knew the man who had taken it; had followed him thousands of miles. Now there had come to her a man of her own race, who assured her that the treasure was not in the possession of the man who had stolen it, but in the possession of an honest man who would willingly surrender it to her, providing only he could be made certain that it was to go directly into her hands. That this might be, he demanded that she meet him at a certain place known to the strange Japanese. There she might prove her property. The story did seem plausible—and her need was great. Soon she would be cast out upon the world without a penny. So long as she had money she was welcome at this club; not longer.

There came the purring of a muffled bell in the hall. He had come.

Should she go? A mood of reckless desperation seized her.

"I will," she declared.

The next instant she was tucking a short, gleaming blade beneath her silk middy and then drawing on a long silk coat.

The man waited in the hallway. He was doubtless prepared for another extended argument, but none came. Instead, the girl walked down the steps with him and into a waiting taxi.

It was a rather long ride they took. First speeding along between rows of apartment houses they at last dashed into the business section of the city. The stranger sat in one corner of the cab, not saying a word. Passing through the business section, they approached the river. It was then that Cio-Cio-San's heart began to be filled with dread. She had heard of many dark deeds done down by the river. But after all, what could they want of her, a poor Japanese girl, almost without funds?

The cab came to a stop with a jolt. A tall building loomed above them. The strange Japanese held the door open that she might alight. She stepped to the sidewalk, and, at that instant, strong arms seized her, pinning her arms to her sides, while a coarse cloth was drawn tightly over her mouth. She then felt herself being pushed through space, and the next moment heard the muffled echoes of the footsteps of her captors. They were in the basement of some great deserted building, the sound told her that.

"Betrayed! Betrayed!" her mind kept repeating. "Betrayed by one of my own people!"

CHAPTER XVII

A THREE-CORNERED BATTLE

While Johnny and Hanada were being led away to the patrol box a young man came running up. He was a reporter, out scouting for news.

"Who's that?" he asked, as he caught a glimpse of Johnny's face.

"Johnny Thompson, you nut!" growled the policeman. "Didn't you never view that map of his before?"

"Yes, but Johnny Thompson's dead."

"All right, have it your own way."

"What's the charge?"

"Conspiracy. Now beat it."

The youth started on a run for the nearest telephone. He had hit upon a first page story. A half-hour later every newsboy in the downtown district was shouting himself hoarse, and the words he shouted were these:

"All about Johnny Thompson. Johnny Thompson, featherweight champion. Alive! Arrested for conspiracy! Extry!"

The theatre crowds were thronging the streets, and the newsies reaped a rich harvest. Among those in the throng was Mazie Mortimer, Johnny Thompson's onetime pal. She had gone to the theatre alone. When Johnny was in Chicago, she had gone with him, but now no one seemed to quite take his place.

As she hastened to the elevated station the shouts of the newsboys struck her ears. At first she heard only those two electrifying words, "Johnny Thompson." Then she listened and heard it all.

Had she not been held up and hurried along by the throng, she would have fallen in a faint. As it was her senses seemed to reel. "Johnny Thompson! Alive! Arrested! Conspiracy!" It could not be true.

Breaking away from the crowd, she snatched a paper from a boy, flung him a half-dollar, then hurried to the corner, where, beneath an arclight she read the astounding news. Again it seemed that her senses would desert her. With an effort she made her way to a restaurant where a cup of black coffee revived her.

For a time she sat in a daze, utterly oblivious of the figure she cut—a well dressed, handsome young woman in opera cloak and silk gown, seated at the counter of a cheap restaurant.

Johnny Thompson alive, here in Chicago, arrested for conspiracy? What did it mean? Could it mean that Johnny had been a deserter, that he had become involved in the radical movement which, coming from Russia, seemed about to sweep the country off its feet? She could not quite believe that, but—

Suddenly a new thought sent her hurrying into the street. Hailing a taxi, she ordered the chauffeur to drive around the block until she gave him further orders. Her thoughts now were all shaped toward a definite end: Johnny Thompson, her good pal, was not dead. He was in Chicago and in trouble. If it were within her power, she must find him and help him.

Studying the newspaper, she noted the point at which he had been arrested. "Wells street bridge," she read. "That means the Madison Street police station."

Her lips were at the speaking tube in an instant. "Madison Street police station, and hurry!" she ordered. "An extra five for speed." The taxi whirled around a corner on two wheels; it shot by a policeman; dodged up an alley, and out on the other side, then stopped with a jolt that came near sending Mazie through the glass.

"Here you are." She thrust a bill in the driver's hand, then raced up the steps and into the forbidding police station.

A sergeant looked up from the desk as she entered.

"Johnny Thompson," she said excitedly. "I want to see Johnny Thompson!"

"I'd like to myself, miss," he said smiling. "There never was a featherweight like him. But he's dead."

"Dead?" Mazie caught at her throat.

"Sure. Didn't you read about it? Long time ago. Died in Russia."

"Oh!" Mazie sank limply into a chair. "Then you haven't heard? He isn't arrested? He isn't here?"

"Arrested?" The sergeant's face took on an amused and puzzled look; then he smiled again. "Oh, yes, there was something on the records tonight saying he and a Jap was wanted for conspiracy. But take it from me, lady, that's all pure bunk; some crook posing as Johnny Thompson, more than likely. I tell you, there never was a more loyal chap than this same Johnny; one of the first to enlist."

"I—I know," faltered Mazie. Now, for the first time, she noticed a man who had entered after her. He stepped to the desk and asked a question regarding a person she knew nothing of. Then he went silently out again. Mazie sat quite still, then rising, she smiled faintly at the sergeant.

"I—I guess you must be right—but—but the papers are full of it."

"Oh, the papers!" The officer spread his hands out in a gesture of contempt. "They'd print anything!"

As Mazie stepped out into the street she was approached by a man, and with a little start, she noticed that it was the one who had entered the police station a few minutes before. Halting, she waited for him to speak.

"You were looking for Johnny Thompson?" He said the words almost in a whisper.

"Yes."

"Well, he is alive. He is not dead. He was arrested, but has been discharged. I can take you to him. Shall I?"

"Oh, will you?" Mazie's voice echoed her gratitude.

"Sure. There's a taxi now," the man replied in a foreign accent.

* * * * *

Johnny had not been released; far from it. And yet it was true, he was at that very moment free. His freedom was only from moment to moment, however; the kind of freedom one gets who runs away from the police.

It was not Johnny's fault that he ran away either. They had been following the orders of the police to the letter, he and Hanada. They had gone across the bridge with them, had meekly submitted to being handcuffed, had been waiting for the patrol-wagon, when things happened.

Four men dashed suddenly from the darkness, and before the patrolmen could draw guns or clubs, before Johnny could realize what was happening, the officers were flat on the pavement, with hands and feet tied. Johnny's brain worked rapidly. He understood all right. These men were Radicals. He was the prize they were after—he and the diamonds. Once let him be taken to the police station, there to be searched, the diamonds would be lost to them forever.

But handcuffed as he was, Johnny was not the boy to submit to being kidnapped without a fight. As one of the Radicals leaped at him, he put his hands up, as in a sign of surrender, then brought them, iron bracelets and all, crashing down on the fellow's head. The man went down without a cry.

Hanada, too, had not been idle. He slipped the handcuffs from his slender wrists and seizing the club of one of the fallen policemen, aimed a blow at the second man who leaped at Johnny. A moment later, Johnny heard his shrill whisper:

"C'mon!"

They were away like a flash. Down a dark alley, over a fence, with Johnny's handcuffs jangling, they sped. Then, after crossing a street and leaping into a yard filled with junk and scrap iron, they paused.

"Let's see," said Hanada.

He took Johnny's wrist, and after twisting the iron bracelets and working for a moment with a bit of rusty wire, he unlocked the handcuffs and threw them in the scrap heap.

"Clumsy things! Belong there," he grunted.

"But," said Johnny slowly, "what's the big idea? They'll get us again, and running away will only get us in bad. They'll think those Radicals were in cahoots with us."

"I think not," said Hanada. "We left them one or two of the Radicals for samples. But that doesn't much matter now. They will get me, yes. And they will not let me go either, not even under bond. But you, you have done nothing. They will let you go. My testimony will set you free. Then you must carry on the hunt and the fight, which they will keep me from continuing because they do not know what they are doing. That's why I must have a little time to talk to you before they take me; time to explain everything, and to tell you how very important it is that you get that Russian, and all those that are with him."

"My room," whispered Johnny, now breathless with interest. "My room; the police do not know about it. We might be able to hide there for hours. We can reach it by the next bridge and by alleys and roofs. C'mon!"

CHAPTER XVIII

HANADA'S SECRET

Johnny smiled grimly. He was in his old place by the window overlooking the river. Hanada was seated beside him.

They could hear the many noises that rose from the street below. Now a patrol wagon came jangling by. Now a squad of policemen emerged from one alley to plunge down another. A riot call had been sent in and the streets were alive with patrolmen and detectives all on the trail of Johnny and his Japanese companion. By this time, too, they must be on the trail of the Radicals. So far as Johnny knew, the Radicals had not actually interfered with the enforcement of the law. Now driven to desperation at the thought of the loss of that treasure which was still in Johnny's possession, they had stepped over the line. From now on the police would be after them. Johnny was awakened from these reflections by the voice of Hanada.

"That man," the Japanese youth was saying, "that Russian, the one we have followed so far, he is the big one, the head of the Radical movement, and he is at this moment in conference with all his chosen leaders. To-morrow, next day, next week, he may strike. And what will the result be? Who can tell? In the whole world he has millions of followers who will rise at his call. We must get him, get that man before it is too late. I am a member of the Japanese Secret Police. And you?"

"A plain American citizen," answered Johnny, "which, by the laws of our land, makes me a policeman, a marshal, a member of the secret service—anything and everything, when the safety of my people, the stability of my government, is at stake." Johnny's chest swelled proudly.

"Oh! I understand," breathed Hanada.

"But," said Johnny quickly, "you say we must get that man. I have had opportunities to kill him, to let him be killed and always you have hindered me. Why?"

"Don't you see even now?" Hanada asked. "Don't you see that now is the time to strike? Now he is meeting with his leaders. We must take him not alone, but the whole band. We must scatter them to the ends of the earth, put them in prison, banish them. Then the whole affair will be ended forever."

Hanada leaned forward. His eyes glowed; his words were sharp with excitement. Johnny listened, breathless.

"We must get them all," he continued. "That is why our secret service people allowed him to break through the lines at Vladivostok, and make his way north to cross the Strait. That is why I followed him, as an Eskimo, to dog his tracks and yet to protect him. That is why he could not be killed. He was to be a decoy; a decoy for the whole band. Your Secret Service, of which I thought you were a member, would not have allowed him to cross to America. That is why I deserted you at East Cape. I thought you were of the Secret Service, and would have the Russian arrested as soon as his foot touched American soil. That is why I said the offer of a reward for his arrest was a blunder. Don't you see? We were to get them all."

"But the girl, Cio-Cio-San?" Johnny questioned.

"She is not of the secret police. She helps me as a friend, that's all, and I will help her if I can."

Johnny wished to question him regarding the treasure, but something held him back.

"So you see how it is." Hanada spoke wearily. "We have gone so far, so very far. Mebbe to-morrow, mebbe next day, we would have uncovered their lair; but to-night the police are on my trail, for 'treason' they call it. Bah! It was a dream, a great and wonderful dream; a dream that would mean much for your country and mine." His words were full of mystery. "But now they will arrest me, and you must carry on the hunt for the Russian and his band. This other thing, it can wait. It will come, sometime, but not now."

"What other?" asked Johnny.

Hanada did not answer.

There came the stealthy shuffle of feet in the corridor.

"They are coming," whispered Hanada. "Remember my testimony will free you, but you must not stop; you must hunt as never before, you must get that man!"

There came, not the expected tattoo of police billies on the door, but a shrill whisper through the key-hole:

"Johnny," the voice said, "are you there? Let me in. I seen it! I seen it! I get the century note you promised me! Let me in!"

*   *   *   *   *

When Mazie entered the taxi with the man who was an entire stranger to her she did it on the impulse of the moment. The swift sequence of events had carried her off her feet. First, she had been startled into the hope that Johnny still lived; then she had been assured by the police sergeant that he could not possibly be living, only to be told a moment later by this stranger that he was still alive.

Once she had settled back against the cushions and felt the jolt of the taxi over the car tracks, she began to have misgivings. Was this a trap? Had she better call to the driver and demand to be allowed to alight? A glance at her fellow traveler tended to reassure her. He was undoubtedly a foreigner, but was an honest-looking fellow and neatly dressed.

As the cab lurched into a side street toward the river, she again experienced misgivings; but this time it was the faint hope still lingering in her breast of seeing her good pal once more that kept her in her seat.

The taxi paused before an old building which was enshrouded in darkness. She was ushered out of the taxi and the next instant, before she had time to cry out, she was bound and gagged. Her feet were tied as well as her hands, and she was hastily carried into the building. Through rooms and halls all dark as night she was half carried, half dragged, until she found herself out over the swirling waters of the river.

Wild questions rushed through her brain. Was this murder? Bound and gagged as she was, would she be thrown into the river to drown? Why? Who were these men? She had not believed until that moment that she had an enemy in the world. She knew no secrets that could inspire anyone to kill her.

While all these thoughts were driving through her brain, she was being slowly lowered toward the water. Down, down she sank until it seemed to her she could feel the wash of the water on her skirts. At that instant, when all seemed lost, strong arms seized her and she was carried down a clanking iron stairway. She caught her breath. She must now be far below the level of the water. What place was this she was being taken into? And why?

She was finally flung down upon a leather covered lounge. The next moment the whole place seemed to be sinking with her as if she were in some slowly descending elevator.

Opening her eyes she looked about her. The place, a long and narrow compartment, was dimly lighted by small incandescent bulbs. The trapdoor, or whatever it had been, through which she had been carried, was closed.

Eight or ten men were grouped about the room, while in one of the darkest corners cowered a little Japanese girl. One of the men came close to Mazie and untied her bonds, also removing the gag. She was now free to move and talk. She realized the utter uselessness of either. The walls of the room appeared to be of steel. There was a strange stuffiness about the air of the place; they must be either underground or under water. She did not know what was to be the next move, or why she was here. She realized only that she could do nothing.

Instinctively she moved toward the girl in the corner. Before she had gone half the distance, a man uttered a low growl of disapproval, and motioned her to a chair. She sat down unsteadily and, as she did so, she realized that the place had a slightly rolling motion, like a ship on the sea.

CHAPTER XIX

"I SEEN IT—A SUBMARINE!"

When Johnny realized that it was Jerry the Rat who was whispering at the keyhole he admitted him at once.

"I seen it! I seen it; a submarine! A German submarine in the river!" the Rat whispered excitedly. "I seen dose blokes wid me own eyes. Dey wuz packin' a skirt thru de hatch. Den dey dropped in too. Den dey let down the hatch, an' swush-swuey, down she went, an' all dey left was a splash in de ol' Chicago!"

"A submarine!" Johnny exclaimed. "That doesn't sound possible; not a German submarine surely!"

"The same," insisted Jerry. "Some old tub. Saw her over by the Municipal Pier, er one like her. Some old fish!"

Johnny sat in silent thought. Hanada was gazing out of the window. Suddenly the Jap exclaimed in surprise:

"Did you see that? There it goes again! Lights flashing beneath the water. It's the 'sub' for sure. Couldn't be anything else."

"I have seen such lights before," said Johnny, striving hard to maintain a sane judgment in this time of great crisis, "but I attributed it to phosphorus on the water."

"Couldn't be!" declared Hanada. "Couldn't make a flicker and flash like that. I tell you, it's a submarine, and the home of the Radicals. That's why we couldn't find them. That's where our Russian disappeared to that night on the bridge. That's where the shots came from. Remember right from the center of the river? That's where your four assailants went to when they vanished from that deserted building. It's the Radicals. C'mon! We may not be too late yet. We'll get them before the police get us."

Together the three rushed from the room.

"Did you say they were carrying a woman?" Johnny asked Jerry, as they hastened down the stairs.

"Yes, a skirt; a swell-looking skirt. Mouth gagged, hands tied, but dressed to kill, opry coat and everything!"

"Some more of their dirty work," Johnny grumbled, "but we'll get them this time. If we can convince the police that they're there they'll drag the river and haul 'em out like a dead rat."

*   *   *   *   *

At the moment when the three men were hurrying down the stairs which led from Johnny's room to the street, Mazie sat silently searching the faces of the men about her. Wild questions raced through her brain. Who were these men? Why had they kidnapped her? What did they want? What would they do to her? She shivered a little at the last question.

That they were criminals she had not the least doubt. Only criminals could do such a thing. But what type of criminal were they? In her research courses at the University she had visited court rooms, jails and reformatories. Criminals were not new to her. But these men lacked utterly the markings of the average city criminal. Their eyes lacked the keen alertness, their fingers the slim tapering points of the professional crook. Suddenly, as she pondered, there came to her mind a paragraph from one of her text-books on crime:

"There are two types of law-breakers. The one believes that the hand of organized society is lifted against him; the other that he is bound to lift his hand against organized society. The first class are the common crooks of the street, and are oft-times more to be pitied than blamed, for after all, environment has been a great factor in their undoing. The second group are those men who are opposed to all forms of organized society. They are commonly known as Radicals. There is little to be said in their favor. Reared, more often than not, in the lap of a society organized for the welfare of all, they turn ungratefully against the mother who nurtured and protected them."

As she recalled this, Mazie realized that this group must be a band of Radicals. Radicals? And one of them had promised to take her to her friend, Johnny Thompson. Could it be that in Russia, that hotbed of radicalism, Johnny had had his head turned and was at that moment a member of this band? It did not seem possible. She would not for a moment believe it.

She was soon to see, for a man of distinctly Russian type, a short man with broad shoulders, sharp chin and frowning brow, approached her, and in a suave manner began to speak to her.

"You have nothing to fear from us, Miss," he began. "We are gentlemen of the finest type. No harm will come to you during your brief stay with us; and I trust it may be very brief."

Mazie heaved a sigh of relief. Perhaps there was going to be nothing so very terrible about the affair after all.

"We only ask a little service of you," the Russian continued as he let down a swinging table from the wall, and drawing a chair to it, motioned her to be seated. He next placed pen, ink and paper on the table.

"You cannot know," he said with a smile, "that your friend, Johnny Thompson, has been causing me a very great deal of trouble of late."

Mazie felt a great desire to shout on hearing this, for it told her plainly that Johnny was no friend of this crowd.

"No, of course you could not know," the man went on, "since you have not seen him. I may say frankly that your friend is clever, and has a way, quite a way, of using his hands."

Mazie did not need to be told that.

"But it is not that of which I wish to speak." The Russian took a step nearer. Mazie, feeling his hot breath on her cheek, shrank back. "Your friend, as I say, has been troubling us a great deal, and in this he has been misled, sadly misled. He does not understand our high and lofty purpose; our desire to free all mankind from the bonds of organized society. If he knew he would act far differently. Of course, you cannot explain all this to him, but you can write him a note, just a little note. You will write it now, in just another moment. First, I will tell you what to say. Say to him that you are in great trouble and danger. Say that you may be killed, or worse things may happen to you, unless he does precisely as you tell him to do. Say that he is to leave a certain package, about which he knows well enough, at the Pendergast Hotel, to be given to M. Kriskie. Say that he is, after that, to leave Chicago at once and is not to return for sixty days.

"See?" He attempted another smile. "It is little that we ask of you; little that we ask of him—virtually nothing."

Mazie's heart was beating wildly. So that was the game? She was to be a decoy. She knew nothing of Johnny's actions, but knew they were for the good of his country. How could she ask him to abandon them for her sake?

As her eyes roamed about the room they fell upon the little Jap girl. In her face Mazie read black rage for the Russian, and a deep compassion for herself.

"Come," said the Russian; "we are wasting time. Is it not so? You must write. You should begin now. So, it will be better for all."

For answer, Mazie took the paper in her white, delicate fingers and tore it across twice. Then she threw it on the floor.

Quickly the man's attitude changed to wild rage.

"So!" he roared. "You will not write? You will not? We shall see!"

He seized her arm and gripped it until the blood rushed from her face, and she was obliged to bite her lips to suppress a scream.

"So!" he raged. "We shall see what happens to young women like you. First, we will kill your young friend, Johnny Thompson; then what good will your refusal have done? After that, we shall see what will happen to you. We Radicals will win by fair means or foul. What does it matter what means we take, so long as the point has been won?"

Roughly he pulled her from the chair and flung her from him.

Then the little Japanese girl was dragged to the chair. A Japanese man, whom Mazie had not before noticed, came forward. From his words and gestures Mazie concluded that he was going through, in the Japanese language, the same program which the Russian had just finished.

The results were apparently the same, for at the close the girl threw the paper cm the floor and stamped upon it. At that the Russian's rage knew no bounds. With an imprecation, he sprang at the Japanese girl. As Mazie looked on in speechless horror, she fancied she caught the gleam of a knife in the girl's hand.

But at that instant the attention of all was drawn to a man, who, after peering through some form of a periscope for a moment, had uttered a surprised exclamation. Instantly the Japanese man sprang to a strangely built rifle which lay against the wall. This he fitted into a frame beside the periscope and thrust its long barrel apparently through the ceiling of the compartment and into the water above. Adjusting a lever here, and another there, he appeared to sight through a hollow tube that ran along the barrel.

"Now," said the Russian, a cruel gleam in his eye, "we shall kill your two friends whom you so blindly refused to protect. Providence has thrown them within our power. They are on the bridge at this moment. The rifle, you see, protrudes quite through the water. Our friend's aim is true."

The Japanese girl, seeming to grasp the import of this, sprang at her fellow countryman. But she was too late. There came the report of two explosions in quick succession. Through the periscope, Mazie caught a glimpse of two bodies falling on the bridge. Then she closed her eyes. Her senses reeled.

This lasted but a moment. Then her eyes were on the little Jap girl. She had dropped to the floor, as if crushed; but there was a dark gleam of unutterable hate in her eyes. She was looking at the Japanese man, who, after firing the rifle, had turned and was going through a door into a rear compartment.

Like a flash, the Jap girl sprang after him. With a cry that died on her lips, Mazie followed, and as she entered the compartment slamming the heavy metal door, she threw down the iron clamps which held it.

They were now two to one, but that one was a man. However, there was no call for effort on her part. Like a tigress the Japanese girl, Cio-Cio-San, sprang at the man of her own country.

"You traitor!" she gasped. "You have betrayed me, your fellow-countryman, and murdered my friend!" and she drove her dagger into his breast to the hilt.

Mazie closed her eyes and sat down dizzily. When she dared look up, she saw the man sprawled on the floor, and the girl crouching beside him, like a wild beast beside her kill.

Seeming to feel Mazie's eyes upon her, Cio-Cio-San turned and smiled strangely, as she said:

"He is dead!"

CHAPTER XX

AT THE BOTTOM OF THE RIVER

The Russian had told the truth when he said the friends of Mazie and Cio-Cio-San were on the bridge. Johnny and Hanada had rushed from the room and had been standing there straining their eyes for a trace of that strange light beneath the water, when the first shot rang out. But the Russian had not counted on the extraordinary speed with which Johnny could drop to earth.

Before the second shot could be fired, Johnny was flat on the surface of the bridge, quite out of range. Hanada had not fared so well. The first shot had been aimed at him and had found its mark. He lay all crumpled up, groaning in mortal agony.

"Get you?" Johnny whispered.

"Yes," the boy groaned, "but you—you get that man."

There came the tramp of feet on the bridge. The police had heard the shots. The long finger of light from the police boat again felt its way back and forth through the darkness.

"D' you shoot?" demanded the first policeman to arrive.

"No! No! They didn't do it," a second man interrupted before Johnny could reply. "It came from the river. I saw the flash. Devils of the river's deep! What kind of a fight is this, anyway?"

"I seen it! I seen it!" It was Jerry the Rat who now broke into the gathering throng. "I seen it; a German sub."

"A submarine!" echoed a half dozen policemen at once.

"I think he is right," said Johnny. "You better drag the river."

"Hello!" exclaimed one of the officers. "If this ain't the same two guys we've been looking for? Johnny Thompson and the Jap."

"You are right," said Johnny disgustedly, "but for once use a little reason. There are world crooks down there in the river and they have some helpless woman there as hostage. Perhaps by this time they may be killing her. I'll keep. I can't get away; not for good. I'm known the country over, beside your charge against me is false, idiotic."

"Yes, yes," it was Hanada's hoarse whisper. "Take me to a hospital. I'll tell all and you will know he was not in it at all. Let him help you. And—and, for God's sake, get that man."

He sank back unconscious.

"Here, Mulligan," ordered a sergeant, "you and Murphy take this Jap to the Emergency quick. You, Kelly and Flannigan, get over to the box and call the police boats with drags. Tell 'em to drag the river from Madison street in one direction and from the lake in the other. It sounds like a dream, but this thing has got to be cleared up. Them shots come from the river sure's my name's Harrigan. We got to find how it's done."

A half hour later, two innocent looking police boats moved silently up the river from Madison street bridge. They traveled abreast, keeping half the river's width between them. From their bows there protruded to right and left, heavy iron shafts. From these iron shafts, at regular intervals, there hung slender but strong steel chains. These chains reaching nearly to the bottom of the river were fitted up at the lower end with heavy pronged steel hooks. At that same moment, two similarly equipped boats started up the river from the lake. They were combing the river with a fine tooth comb.

*   *   *   *   *

Meanwhile the men beneath the surface of the river were not idle. They did not realize the danger which their last act had drawn them into and therefore did not attempt to escape by running their craft out into the lake. But they did have other matters to attend to. One of their number was locked in the rear compartment. His fate was unknown to them. This much they did know, he had not unfastened the door nor answered when they called to him.

After vainly pounding and kicking the door, they lifted a heavy steel shaft and using this as a battering ram, proceeded to smash the door from its fastenings. At first this did not avail. But at last each succeeding blow left a slightly larger gap between the door and its steel jamb. Then suddenly, after a violent ram, which sent echoes through the compartment, the lower catch gave way. With a hoarse shout the Russian urged his men to redoubled effort. Three more times they backed away to come plunging forward. The third blow struck the door at the very spot where the fastening still hung. And then, with a creaking groan the door gave way.

Just inside the door, Mazie stood tense, motionless, her arms outstretched in terror. Fingers rigid, lips half-parted in a scream, she stared at the door. In the doorway stood the Russian, a knife gleaming in his hand. For a second his eyes searched the room. Then they fell on the body of the Jap huddled on the floor. Rage darkened his face as the Russian took a step forward.

At that instant there had come a dull sound of metal grating on metal. The Russian toppled over on his side and the two girls were thrown to the floor.

The chamber had given a sudden lurch. The next instant it rolled quite over, piling the two women and the corpse in a heap and sending the door shut with a bang. The Russian had fallen outside. The craft rolled over, once, twice, three times and then hung there, with the floor for its ceiling.

Overcome with fright and misery, Mazie did not stir for a full minute, then she dragged herself from the gruesome spot where she lay.

She gave one quick glance at the door. It appeared to have been wedged solidly shut. Then she turned to Cio-Cio-San, who also had arisen.

"What can have happened?" Mazie asked in a voice she could scarcely believe was her own.

What had happened was this: one of the hooks on the police boat had caught in an outer railing of the submarine. The giant iron fish was hooked.

To throw other drags, fastened on longer chains, into the sub; to send tugs and police boats snorting backward; to tighten the chains and draw the sub to the surface, to whirl it about until the hatchway was once more at the upper side, this was merely a matter of time.

When the Radicals saw what had been done, they doubtless realized that if they refused to come out the lid would be blown off and they would be likely to perish in the explosion. They had apparently planned to charge the police and attempt an escape, for the Russian came first with a rush, a pistol in each hand. But Johnny Thompson's good right arm spoiled all this. He had leaped to the surface of the sub and when the Russian appeared he gave him a blow under the chin that lifted him off his feet and sent him plunging into the river.

Seeing this the other members of the gang surrendered.

Johnny was the first man below. Seeing the closed door to the right, he hammered on it, shouting:

"C'mon out, we're the police."

Slowly the door opened. There before him stood Mazie.

"Mazie!" Johnny's eyes bulged with astonishment.

"Johnny!" There was a sob in her voice. Then catching herself, she glanced down at her wrinkled and blood-bespattered dress.

"Johnny," she implored, "for goodness' sake get me out of this horrid place so I can change these clothes."

"There's decent enough dresses at the police station," suggested a smiling officer.

"Call the wagon," said Johnny.

Soon they were rattling away toward the station, Mazie, Cio-Cio-San, and Johnny.

"Johnny," Mazie whispered, "you didn't desert, did you?"

"Did you think that?" Johnny groaned in mock agony.

"No, honest I didn't, but what—what did you do?"

"Just got tired of waiting for Uncle Sam to bring me home from Russia, so I walked, that's all. Here's my discharge papers, all right. And here's my transportation."

With a smile Johnny handed her the two crumpled papers.

"You see," he exclaimed, "a Russian brigand got me in the left arm when I was guarding the Trans-Siberian Railroad. They sent me to the hospital, then gave me my discharge. Said I'd be no more good as a soldier. And after waiting for a boat that never seemed to come I hit out for the north. Nothing crooked about that at all, but I had to be a bit sly about it anyway, for Uncle Sam don't like to have you take chances even if you are discharged."

"Oh! Johnny, that's grand!" murmured Mazie.

The rest of the journey was accomplished in silence. Now and again Mazie gave Johnny's arm a little squeeze, as if to make sure he was still there.

"Gee, kid," Johnny exclaimed as Mazie reappeared, after a half hour in the matron's room. "You sure do look swell."

She was dressed in the plain cotton dress furnished by the city to destitute prisoners. But the dress was as spotlessly clean as was Mazie's faultless complexion.

"Gee, Mazie!" Johnny went on, "I've seen you in a lot of glad rags but this tops them all. Looks like you'd just come from your own kitchenette."

Mazie bit her lip to hide her confusion. Then blushing, she said:

"Johnny, I'm hungry. When do we eat?"

"I know a nice place right round the corner. C'mon. Where's Cio-Cio-San?"

"Gone to the Emergency hospital."

"Hanada," Johnny exclaimed. "I must find out about him."

"Just came from there myself," said the police sergeant, a kindly light in his eyes. "I'm sorry to tell you, but your friend's checked in."

"Dead?"

"Dead," answered the officer, "but he lived long enough to know that the band of world outlaws was captured. He died happy knowing that he had served his country well, and I guess that's about all any Jap asks."

"Oh, yes, one more thing," he went on; "he cleared up that little matter of conspiracy before he died. Something that concerned him alone. You weren't in it. His part, well, you might call it treason, then again you mightn't. Considering what he's done for this country and his, we don't call it treason. It's been sponged off the slate."

"I'm glad to hear that," sighed Johnny, as he turned to rejoin Mazie.

CHAPTER XXI

THE OWNER OF THE DIAMONDS

Johnny did not return to his room that night. After reporting to the police station and letting them know where he might be found if needed, he secured a room in one of Chicago's finest hotels, and pulling down the blinds turned in to sleep until noon.

When he awoke he remembered at once that he had several little matters to attend to. Hanada's funeral would be cared for by his own people. But he must see Cio-Cio-San; he must get the hundred dollars promised to Jerry the Rat and he must put in a claim for the thousand dollars reward offered for the arrest of the Russian. He need bother his head no longer about the captured Radicals. There was plenty of evidence aboard the craft to condemn them to prison or deportation.

When he came down to the hotel desk he found a letter waiting for him. He opened this in some surprise and read it in great astonishment. It was from one of Chicago's richest men; a man he had never met and indeed had never dreamed of meeting. Yet here was the man's note requesting him to meet him in his private office at five o'clock.

"All right, I'll do that little thing," Johnny whispered to himself, "but meantime I'll go out to the University and see Cio-Cio-San."

An hour later he found himself sitting beside the Japanese girl on the thick mats of that Japanese room at her club.

"Cio-Cio-San," he said thoughtfully, "I remember hearing you tell of having been robbed of a treasure. Did you find it last night in the submarine?"

"No," she said softly. "Last night was a bad night for me. I lost my best friend. He is dead. I lost my treasure. I do not hope to ever find it now."

"Cio-Cio-San," Johnny said the name slowly. "Since you do not hope ever to see your treasure again, perhaps you will tell me what it was."

"Yes, I will tell you. You are my good friend. It was diamonds, one hundred and ten diamonds and ten rubies, all in a leather lined envelope with three long compartments. The rubies were at the bottom of the envelope."

"Then," said Johnny, "you are not so far from your treasure after all. A few of the stones are gone, but most of them are safe."

He drew from his pocket the envelope which he had carried so far and at such great peril.

Had he needed any reward, other than the consciousness of having done an honest deed, he would have received it then and there in the glad cry that escaped from the Japanese girl's lips.

When she had wept for joy, she opened the envelope and shaking out the three loose stones dropped them into Johnny's hand.

"What's that?" he asked.

"A little reward. A present."

Taking the smallest of the three between finger and thumb he gave her back the others.

"One is enough," he told her. "I'll give it to Mazie."

"Ah, yes, to Mazie, your so beautiful, so wonderful friend," she murmured. Then, after a moment, "As for me, I go back to my own people. I shall spend my life and my fortune helping those very much to be pitied ones who have lost all in that so terrible Russia."

As Johnny left that room, he thought he was going to have that diamond set in a ring and present it to Mazie the very next day. But he was not. That interview with one of Chicago's leading bankers at five o'clock was destined to change the course of his whole life; for though the Big Five had never decided to act in unison with Hanada in his wild dream of a Kamchatkan Republic—the plan which had brought his arrest as a conspirator—they did propose to work those Kamchatkan gold mines on an old concession, given them by the former Czar, and they did propose that Johnny take charge of the expedition.

THE END.

Printed in the United States
41653LVS00016B/49